# ANDY BRIGGS
# HERO.COM

# Crisis
# Point

# OXFORD
UNIVERSITY PRESS

Great Clarendon Street, Oxford OX2 6DP
Oxford University Press is a department of the University of Oxford.
It furthers the University's objective of excellence in research, scholarship,
and education by publishing worldwide in

Oxford   New York

Auckland   Cape Town   Dar es Salaam   Hong Kong   Karachi
Kuala Lumpur   Madrid   Melbourne   Mexico City   Nairobi
New Delhi   Shanghai   Taipei   Toronto

With offices in

Argentina   Austria   Brazil   Chile   Czech Republic   France   Greece
Guatemala   Hungary   Italy   Japan   Poland   Portugal   Singapore
South Korea   Switzerland   Thailand   Turkey   Ukraine   Vietnam

Oxford is a registered trade mark of Oxford University Press
in the UK and in certain other countries

British Library Cataloguing in Publication Data

Data available

ISBN: 978-0-19-272925-5

1 3 5 7 9 10 8 6 4 2

Printed in Great Britain by Clays Ltd, St Ives plc

Paper used in the production of this book is a natural,
recyclable product made from wood grown in sustainable forests.
The manufacturing process conforms to the environmental
regulations of the country of origin.

A huge thanks to a real super-team:
Polly, Julian, Anna, Liz, Helen, Molly
and the rest of the OUP gang too numerous
to mention but too precious to forget!

From: Andy Briggs
To: HERO.COM readers everywhere
Subject: Careful on the web!

As you know, the Internet is a brilliant invention, but you need to be careful when using it.

In this awesome book, the heroes (and villains!) stumble across the different websites accidentally. But HERO.COM and VILLAIN.NET don't really exist. :-(
I thought them up when I was dreaming about how cool it would be if I could fly. The idea for HERO.COM suddenly came to me — especially the scene where Toby and Pete . . . Oh wait! You haven't read it yet so I'd better shut up! :-) Anyway, I began writing and before I knew it, the idea had spiralled into VILLAIN.NET as well. But I had to make up all of the Internet stuff. None of it is really out there on the web.

Here are my tips for safe surfing on the web: keep your identity secret (like all good superheroes do), stick to safe websites, make sure a parent, teacher or guardian knows that you're online — and if anyone sends you anything that makes you feel uncomfortable, don't reply, and tell an adult you trust.

I do have my own website, and it's totally safe (even without superpowers!):
www.whichsideareyouon.co.uk

Be safe out there!

:-)

# CONTENTS

# Bad Feelings

Toby had had a bad feeling from the moment he'd woken up. Now he knew why.

The ground shook as a barrage of energy bolts tore the road apart around them. Cars and lorries were strewn across the autobahn. He, Lorna, and Emily hid behind an overturned truck that still smouldered from the damage it had received. The heavy rain hissed as it came into contact with the vehicle's hot metal surface.

A cow walked by, mooing loudly at Toby, adding a sense of surrealism to the scene. A cattle wagon had been hit, and now fifty confused animals were wandering aimlessly across the battlefield. Toby focused his attention back on the problem at hand.

'We're outnumbered!' he shouted over the noise of car alarms and further explosions. He shivered. He hadn't been counting on travelling the world tonight and was only wearing his jacket and jeans.

'I know that! Do you think I'm blind?' Lorna shouted back, her voice shrill with tension. She gripped the necklace around her neck. It had been a present from her boyfriend, and looked very expensive. He had claimed it was a good luck charm. Lorna hadn't wanted to come on this mission, but as usual her brother had convinced her. She still believed that the Hero Foundation hadn't rewarded them properly for stopping the archfiends Basilisk, Worm, Viral, and Trojan.

Emily peeked round the truck. Their ski-masked opponents had turned their attention to their target—an armoured security truck that lay nose-first in a crater. She counted six villains.

'They must think we're dead. They're trying to open the truck,' she reported.

Toby thought hard. For this mission they had been limited to three superpowers apiece—one transportation, one defensive, and one attack. The limitation was part of the Hero Foundation's restructuring of Hero.com, the website from which they downloaded their superpowers. The Foundation was currently updating its technology. After the destruction of its headquarters, it still couldn't run Hero.com to its full capacity. A fifty per cent reduction was in force across all Downloaders until the system could be completely rebuilt.

*More like interfering than restructuring*, thought Toby bitterly. They were woefully underpowered for this mission, and without Pete fighting by their side, they no longer felt like the super-team they once were.

# Bad Feelings

Toby's mind drifted, wondering how his friend was doing—

The ground shook as the armoured car's doors were blown off. There was a lot of shouting in German. Somebody didn't sound very pleased.

Toby risked a peek, turning on a small device lodged in his ear, impossible to see with a casual glance. The Parser began instantly translating the language.

'You've burnt the money, you idiot!' screamed one of the villains.

Toby grinned as burning euro notes blew past on the breeze. Dumb criminals were his favourite kind.

'Only some of it,' said another thug defensively. 'Look, this lot's fine.'

'We're not here for the cash,' said a female voice. That must be Monika, the one they had been briefed about. 'But grab as much cash as you can, anyway. Look for the black box.'

Lorna nudged Toby's arm. 'It's now or never, while they're distracted.'

Toby nodded. 'Let's take them in a pincer.'

The six villains, all surprisingly short, were hauling heavy money boxes from the back of the van. It took two of them to lift each one.

'Game's over!' yelled Toby as he stepped from cover, all alone.

One of the thugs raised his hands, his fingers glowing

a vibrant orange—but his companion pushed the thug's hands down.

'This one's mine,' said Monika. 'I thought we got rid of you?' she snarled at Toby. The villain took off her skiing mask. Orange-hands did the same.

Toby hesitated. He had been expecting hard-nosed criminals.

'You're . . . just kids?'

Monika took offence at the term 'kid', neatly translated by the Parser, which picked up the vibrations in Toby's larynx and translated his words into whichever language was needed.

'You're a kid yourself,' she snarled.

'You're all Downloaders?' asked Toby in surprise. Their briefing from Hero.com had said the gang were supervillains.

The other thugs took their masks off and looked curiously at Toby.

'He's one of us,' said Orange-hands.

'Is that right?' said Monika with a curious frown. 'You found Villain.net too?'

Toby sighed. Of course, Villain.net: the rival super-power platform to Hero.com. These idiots had obviously fallen for the Council of Evil's annual spamming campaign to lure new recruits.

'Sorry, guys,' said Toby smiling. 'I shop at Hero.com.'

The words penetrated the villains' heads as Toby

# Bad Feelings

spurred forwards, super-fast. He hit the nearest one directly in the chest at sixty miles an hour, hurling him through the air and slamming him into the cattle truck.

Toby skidded several metres on the wet tarmac, crashing into a car, before he could change direction. That was the problem with super-speed; it wasn't like he'd seen in the movies where changing direction was instantaneous. He could run as fast as a bullet but had to slow to almost normal speed before changing direction.

He just had time to trip another crook flat on his back, knocking him out cold, before the others reacted.

To the criminals, Toby was almost a blur moving in perfectly straight lines. They saw two of their friends go down before Monika whipped her arms out—her limbs stretched like rubber and writhed like a snake. Her arms tangled Toby's feet.

Toby crashed to the floor like a wrecking ball. He rolled across the carriageway completely out of control—smashing through the central reservation and into the opposite lanes. Luckily the traffic had halted when the super-thugs had wreaked havoc stopping the security van. Toby lay catching his breath, every part of his body aching.

Lorna and Emily had sprung from cover the moment

Toby had moved into action. By the time Monika had tripped Toby, Lorna had clambered up the rear access ladder of a tanker that had jack-knifed across the road. From there she fired her first shots, a series of glass arrows that swished through the air. Whatever they touched turned instantly to crystal.

The first few hit the security van, which immediately crystallized with an ear-shattering crack. Another clipped Orange-hands as he raised them to shoot. Straight away, the kid turned translucent.

Emily effortlessly bounded over a bus, covering six metres—landing in the middle of the crooks. She jabbed her fingers into one villain's back. He collapsed, fast asleep.

Emily swung for Monika, but the girl lashed out— her rubbery arm lassoing around Emily's hands, drawing them together. Emily hesitated. Monika seized the moment and kicked Emily's elbows—forcing Emily to jab *herself* in the face. The self-inflicted punch delivered the narcoleptic blow. Emily collapsed, instantly out of the fight.

'Em!' screamed Lorna.

Monika ducked as Lorna rained down a volley of glass darts. She leapt sideways, Lorna's missiles turning the ground to crystal behind her. Monika threw herself forward, tumbling like a gymnast, coming to rest behind a cow. Lorna tried to avert her enfilade—but

# Bad Feelings

two darts hit the cow, turning it into solid crystal, cutting off its startled moo. Even though she knew the effect was temporary, Lorna felt guilty about involving the animal.

It was enough of a distraction for the sixth villain to unleash his powers. Superheated air pulsed from his body, exploding on his targets with devastating force. He wasn't aiming for Lorna; he was aiming for the 37,500 litres of petrol in the tanker beneath her feet!

Toby looked up in time to see the tanker truck explode in a brilliant orange mushroom cloud that lit up the autobahn. The blast knocked him backwards and shattered every vehicle window in a hundred-metre vicinity.

'Lorn!' Toby rushed forward, ensuring his super-speed didn't kick in. The last thing he wanted to do was run uncontrollably straight through the tanker inferno. He leaped over the crash barrier, noticing that Monika and her sidekick had grabbed a case and were escaping across the road.

'I got the box!' the boy yelled.

Toby didn't care, the welfare of his sister and Emily was more important.

The vehicles around the blasted tanker were charred and damaged. Emily and the unconscious villains were lying unharmed on the ground protected from the blast by the vehicles they had fallen behind. The crunch of crystal underfoot could only be the remnants of the truck, the poor cow, and—Toby shivered—the crystal-lized villain.

'Lorna?'

He tried to get close to the flames, but the heat was too intense. He felt tears well up, but the flames evapo-rated them. He couldn't lose Lorna. Not after every-thing they had been through.

'Lorna, where are you?' His voice cracked with emo-tion.

'What's the problem?' said a voice from behind.

Toby spun round—Lorna was right there. Toby laughed with relief and felt the urge to hug his sister. Then he came to his senses and in his best peeved tones he said, 'Where did you go?'

'Duh! I teleported before he could shoot me.' She knelt next to Emily and felt for a pulse. 'She's fast asleep.'

The sound of a powerfully revving engine got their attention. On the opposite side of the motorway, the two remaining villains had found a car transporter that had veered off the road. It was full of brand new Porsches—one of which they had hotwired and were now escaping in.

Toby watched the bright red car zip past. Monika was at the wheel, cackling loudly.

# Bad Feelings

'That's so cool!'

'Don't let them get away!' shouted Lorna. 'They have the box!'

Stopping the villains from seizing the box from the armoured car had been their primary mission—although they had no idea what was inside it. As usual their plan was going wrong. They both hesitated for a moment, unsure how to pursue the fiends. Then they looked at each other with the same idea, and the same lopsided grin.

They ran across to the transporter and jumped into the next Porsche, Toby making sure he used a little super-speed to beat his sister to the driver's seat. He released the handbrake and the car rolled smoothly off the transporter.

'We don't have a key,' Lorna said.

Toby scrambled in the glove box, and then behind the sun-visor where the key is always put in films. Nothing. Then he had a bolt of inspiration. He touched the ignition and concentrated on firing a small jolt of his attack power. A spark cracked and the engine roared to life.

'Brilliant!' yelped Lorna. 'Seatbelts!'

Toby pushed the car into gear, as he'd seen his parents do so many times. If they could do it, it must be easy.

The gear engaged with a nasty crunch. He took his

foot off the clutch and braced himself for the ride of his life—

The engine stalled with a wheezy croak. Lorna looked at him in disbelief.

'What did you do?'

'I don't know! It just stalled!'

'Let me try!' She already had her seatbelt off.

'No! I'll try again.'

He tried a second time, and a third. In frustration, Lorna ordered her brother to swap places. But she proved to be no better than he was.

'How hard can this be?' fumed Lorna.

'They're getting away! We better stop messing around and do something.'

Toby sighed, climbed reluctantly out of the sports car, then ran forwards like a rocket.

'That's more like it,' mumbled Lorna.

The two villains pushed the car to its maximum speed of 186 miles per hour. Windscreen-wipers battled rain that was falling so heavily it never cleared from the glass, but they were lucky because the traffic was jammed behind them making the autobahn ahead completely clear.

The boy had wedged the case on the tiny excuse for a backseat. He leaned back and opened it, taking a fist of hundred-euro notes out. He whooped with delight.

'Have you got the black box?' asked Monika urgently.

The boy delved into the case again and handed it over. It was small and long like a pencil case, but with no obvious way of opening it. Monika shook it, but it didn't rattle. She put it on her lap for safety. Retrieving the box is what the mysterious Villain.net had asked her to do in return for her powers and she wasn't going to fail—she was enjoying the night so far. So she'd lost a few of the gang back there, but she hadn't really liked them much anyway. Having downloadable superpowers more than made up for hanging around with a few bored teenagers.

Monika glanced in her rearview mirror and frowned. Something was coming through the cloud of spray kicked up by the sports car. It was difficult to make out exactly what it was because the rain blurred the window. When she looked again their pursuer was gone.

The boy noticed that Monika seemed preoccupied. 'Everything all right?'

She turned to speak to him—and her mouth hung open in astonishment. He followed her gaze to outside *his* passenger window.

Toby was running alongside the car, arms and legs pumping so fast that they were a blur. However, the rest of him was perfectly clear. His head was bowed against the rain that whipped his skin.

'Stop the car!' he yelled.

The girl was so shocked that she slammed on the brakes. The Porsche squealed as it skidded across the wet road. She lost control and the car slewed sideways as it aquaplaned. She tugged the steering wheel hard in the opposite direction—bad idea.

Toby slid to a halt, his feet kicking up a massive curtain of water. He watched as the Porsche spun in circles, grinding to a halt in the centre of the autobahn.

Inside the car it was like being trapped in a washing machine. Euros now plastered the interior. Monika felt sick, and when she looked at her companion she saw he was about to hurl.

'Don't you dare!' she screamed.

Toby walked towards the car, lightning crackling between his fingers as he readied himself for a fight. Lorna teleported next to him with a loud bang.

'You took your time,' he commented drily.

The passenger door opened and the boy was kicked out in a cloud of euro notes and vomit. He looked pitiful. Then the Porsche wheelspun and accelerated straight for an exit ramp.

'I give up,' groaned the kid.

'I'll take care of him,' said Lorna. 'You go after the girl before she kills someone.'

# Bad Feelings

Toby zipped off in pursuit. The Porsche skidded into a busy traffic lane that led into the heart of the city. Toby paused for a second to take in the heavy traffic and the Porsche wildly careering through it, and then shot forwards.

Monika drove at frightening speed, weaving through the traffic always seeming to be centimetres from colliding with other vehicles. She glanced in the rearview mirror and saw that Toby was powering along behind her.

Toby had no idea how he was going to stop the car, but he was thankful he wasn't going full speed so he could still change lanes without too much effort. He gave a brief thought to how this must look to other people, and hoped after a casual glance their eyes would trick them into thinking he was on a motorbike rather than on foot, because superpowers were supposed to be secret.

The Porsche jolted right to avoid a stationary bus. Toby hadn't been paying attention and had to sidestep at the very last moment. Terrified he would trip, instead he found himself sidestepping into the door of the car alongside him. The high-speed impact buckled the side of the vehicle, forcing the driver to slam on the brakes in a cloud of burning rubber. Toby heard the crunch of other vehicles rear-ending the stricken car.

Ahead the Porsche swung round a corner. Toby

slowed down, his trainers skidding across the slick road, swinging him out into the middle of a busy crossroads where the traffic was already in turmoil in the wake of the Porsche.

He was slowly catching up. If he reached out he could grab hold of the spoiler. Monika suddenly changed lanes. Toby followed—

The Porsche passed across a set of tramlines— missing a tram by millimetres. Then something bizarre happened—

Toby's vision shimmered and stretched, as if he was watching events unfold through a distorted funfair mirror. Then it snapped back to normal as *the Porsche passed across a set of tramlines—missing a tram by millimetres—again!*

*Déjà vu.* Toby was so unnerved that he ran straight into the tram.

One side of the tram crunched inwards, glass shattering. Passengers screamed as the tram rocked off its rails and bashed through several cars before toppling over onto its side in a horrendous crash.

Toby rolled from the wreckage unhurt. He was protected from anything more serious than a few scratches by the regeneration power that was now routinely blended with all downloadable powers on Hero.com— all part of the upgraded technology.

He shook his head to clear the wooziness. When he

looked up he saw that the Porsche had stopped at the end of the street. Monika was watching the destruction with a huge smile.

She put the car in gear—and was startled by a bang from the seat next to her. Lorna appeared and snatched the black box from Monika's lap.

'I'll have that!' Then her expression turned to one of disgust. 'Am I sitting in . . . puke?'

Monika extended her arm—and nothing happened. She looked at it in surprise. What had happened to her powers?

'Aw, didn't you know? Those Villain.net powers are knock-offs. They don't last too long. Sorry.'

Monika stamped on the accelerator and the car jerked forwards. Lorna was expecting the move. She reached out and yanked the wheel, aiming straight for the edge of a bridge.

'Are you crazy?' screamed Monika.

The Porsche broke through the barriers, sailed through the air, and splashed into the river.

Toby ran to the bridge to watch the expensive car sink. Lorna appeared next to him with a bang. Toby smiled with relief.

'Where is she?'

Lorna pointed over to two police cars that had finally caught up with the chase. The policemen surrounded a shocked Monika who was cowering on the river bank.

'You teleported out.' Toby was impressed.

'It was a close call. I couldn't teleport with the package. It blocked my powers.'

Toby smelled something unpleasant. 'Urgh! You smell of puke!'

'I don't want to talk about it.'

Toby tried to ignore the smell. 'Where is the package?'

'It's at the bottom of the river,' she said watching the last bubbles rise from the Porsche. 'I'm sure the Foundation can salvage it. At least we stopped those villains from getting their hands on it.'

'We should get back and tell them.'

'First, let's get Em.'

They moved away from the growing crowd, and in a dark side street they teleported back to the armoured truck.

The autobahn destruction looked the same, but Emily had vanished along with the other villains. They combed the area, but could find no trace of their friend. They were forced to stop the search when they heard the sounds of approaching emergency services.

Toby felt a wave of nausea. Something odd was happening. He needed Pete with him more than ever, and,

# Bad Feelings

not for the first time, he wondered how his best friend was doing.

It was the most wonderful feeling Pete could remember experiencing. Everything was going right. Everybody was following orders. Gold bullion glistened in the sun, rising from the pure white sands in perfect stacks. He briefly pondered why the gold was on the beach, but reasoned that it was part of what was turning out to be an unusual day.

Two figures ran across the sands, breathing hard in the noon heat. Their battered costumes did little to cool them down. The pair slumped on their hands and knees, gasping for breath. He was surprised to see them here. He had thought they were both dead.

The first figure looked up, lank black hair pasted to his bone white complexion. At the sight of his distinctive high-browed head, the name came flooding back to Pete. Doc Tempest. The first villain he'd ever fought.

'I have failed you. Please . . . please forgive me! I'm nothing more than a wretch!'

Tempest snivelled like a baby. That made Pete feel even better. He kicked out, marvelling at how muscular his own leg looked. His boot knocked Tempest over; the supervillain groaned and rolled onto his side.

'Failure will not be tolerated!' He roared. His voice possessed a powerful timbre.

The second figure looked up. A heavy cloak, worn around the edges, masked his face. Strong stone hands reached up to the hood as he spoke.

'This is what you wanted,' said Basilisk. 'Wealth, power, control . . . it's all yours to do as you will. It's all within your grasp. You are powerful; *unstoppable.*' The hood fell off and a scarred face looked back. It was a shockingly recognizable face.

It was Pete's own!

'Join us!' demanded Basilisk.

Then blackness. Pete felt his body jerk and a piercing alarm sounded in the distance, a monotonous drone underlining it. Ghostly voices drifted past.

' . . . Massive embolism!'

'He's going to flatline.'

'Clear!'

A thump, louder than the Big Bang, echoed through Pete's skull. Soothing warmth quickly followed it, and the monotonous tone began to dance again.

The annoying voices faded away, and Pete opened his eyes on his new empire once again.

It was everything he had *ever* hoped it would be.

# The Awakening

Next day, Toby was back at school. He couldn't imagine a more wretched place to be. On hearing his report to the Hero Foundation, Eric Kirby, the Foundation's creator and leader, had told Mr Grimm to dispatch a salvage team to collect the black box, although he still hadn't said what was inside it.

Toby and Lorna had also faced a wall of silence about what had happened to Emily. Kirby assured them that she was alive and well, as indicated by her Cellular Uplink Communication Interface—or CUCI, pronounced 'cookie'. It was one of the many new aspects of Hero.com and everybody had to have one. It was essentially a genetic tag that was injected into the wrist and monitored the health, superpower status, and whereabouts of all personnel. It also allowed access to Hero.com from any computer terminal, even without knowing its complex ever-shifting alphanumeric URL. In this case, the CUCI still broadcast Emily's vital signs, although her location could not be pinpointed.

Since Toby and Lorna's old friend Chameleon was

still missing in action, their contact with the Hero Foundation was now Eric Kirby himself. His constant assurances, delivered with his usual unemotional tones, were of no consolation. He had assured them that several Primes—people born with their powers rather than having to download them—were searching for Emily. Her parents had been given a cover story and a mild dose of hypnosis. The Foundation steered clear of full-blown mind control after complications in the past. The best thing Lorna and Toby could do was return home and act normally.

Now at school, Toby felt isolated and alone. He had drifted from his other school friends. Their ordinary lives revolved around TV, games, and football, which didn't compare with travelling the globe and saving the world from peril. Pete was the only friend Toby had left, and Pete was still in hospital. Toby missed him acutely.

Lorna was of no help either. Emily's disappearance had driven her into sullen silences, and she only shared her inner thoughts with her boyfriend, Jake Hunter. Toby dismissed that train of thought. He didn't like Hunter, who was the school bully, and who, Toby realized, was also missing from school. He hadn't been around for the last month. Hopefully he'd finally been expelled.

During a geography lesson, Toby let his mind drift to

# The Awakening

the last time he had spoken to Pete. It was in the Mongolian desert a few weeks ago when they defended the Hero Foundation from the villain Basilisk and his cronies. But the words Pete and Toby had exchanged then had not been very friendly, and that made Toby feel guilty. Pete now lay in a coma at the Foundation's hospital. Toby hated the fact that his last words to his best friend had been harsh ones.

After the Hero Foundation headquarters had crashed into the Mongolian desert, Toby had feared that his superhero adventures would be over, although he was relieved that they had averted Basilisk's plan to seize control of the Hero.com network. He needn't have worried. Back-up facilities around the world had been activated, and the Hero Foundation was currently being rebuilt with all its technological upgrades—at a super-fast pace. Kirby had told Toby, Lorna, and Emily to go home and relax.

Kirby had assured them that Pete was being well looked after, and that he was confident he would recover. But Lorna was furious that they had been sent home without any reward. No fame, no parades, and not a hint of any money for putting their lives on the line. When Toby tried to reason that what they did was for the greater good, she became even angrier. In the argument that followed he had accused his sister of being selfish, while she had accused him of pig-headed stupidity. Emily had tried to stay out of the conversation, but Lorna had sensed her friend was siding with Toby.

'You care more about what you *think* is right than about your own friends, and life,' Lorna had snapped. 'Well, I'm not going on any more missions so you can sacrifice me because you stupidly believe you're doing the right thing! From now on, if the Hero Foundation want me, they can pay me!'

Since then Toby had wondered what he'd do if he was faced with saving his friends or saving the world. He hoped he would never have to find out.

Over the last few weeks, the three friends had regularly visited Pete, but he remained in a deep coma. Mr Grimm had morbidly announced that Pete had technically died on two occasions and had been revived with a defibrillator. The doctors claimed he could hear, but he remained unresponsive. Emily usually cried all the way through the visits, and that made Toby feel even more depressed.

And now she was missing.

During their debriefing last night, Kirby had said that losing the Foundation Headquarters had been a blessing. It was the catalyst needed to rebuild the systems from scratch, using the very latest technology. Kirby had branded the reboot 'Hero.com v2.0'.

Half-listening to the teacher droning on, Toby

wondered what was in the black box Mr Grimm had recovered. Suddenly he wanted to know what they had risked their lives for, what they had lost Emily for.

Thinking about the black box reminded him about the déjà vu he had experienced when chasing Monika. He had meant to tell somebody about it.

Toby's head was filled with unanswered questions.

The school day seemed to stretch into infinity. At lunch he looked for Lorna but couldn't find her. He tried texting and emailing her on his new touch screen mobile phone, another gizmo provided by the Foundation, but she didn't respond. Toby suppressed his anxiety. His sister wasn't missing. She was probably handling the situation in her own way or ignoring him.

The end of the day saw him walking home alone when his mobile vibrated. It was an email from the Foundation. It was an invitation to visit Pete.

As it was an official invitation, it meant that rather than catch a train to the private hospital Pete was in, as he would normally do, Toby could use the teleport power attached to the email. It contained enough digitized power for one use. It was part of the Foundation's new POD service: 'Power on Demand'. Toby smiled, the Foundation seemed to have a new love for acronyms.

He turned into a quiet street and made sure nobody

was watching as he thumbed the attachment and was gone in a small clap of thunder.

The hospital was undergoing some modernization too. Toby appeared on a designated hexagonal pad, opposite the reception desk. The hospital was the Foundation's own, so nobody batted an eyelid when he appeared from nowhere.

The tired nurse behind the desk glanced at a screen that registered Toby's arrival and matched it against a biometric database.

'Ah, Mister Wilkinson. Take the lift to the top floor. Then the third door on your left.'

He made it to Pete's ward on autopilot. Inside, his friend was unconscious, linked to a battery of machinery that was keeping him alive.

During the battle for the Hero Foundation, Pete had faced the arch-villain Basilisk single-handedly. The fight had been brutal and had resulted in Pete being immersed in hundreds of liquid raw superpowers. For a fleeting moment it had given him the strength to defeat Basilisk, but then he had fallen unconscious and had been that way ever since. It was like being exposed to radiation—except nobody knew the consequences of being dipped and smothered in undiluted powers.

Toby glanced around. Nobody else was in the room

and it didn't look as if he'd had any other visitors since Toby was last here. That was sad. Pete didn't have any friends at school and his parents had been kept under hypnosis to prevent them from trying to see their son. Even without the hypnosis, Toby doubted that Pete's parents would bother visiting anyway. The last he'd heard from Pete was that they were separating.

Toby pulled up a chair and tapped Pete's arm, in case he could feel anything.

'Hi, mate. It's Toby, come to see how you are.' It was difficult to keep up a one-sided conversation. He decided it best not to mention that Emily was missing, in case Pete could hear. 'You look . . . the same. I keep expecting to walk in and see you with a big beard.' Toby smiled at the image. 'School was dull, but you'll be pleased to know it looks like Jake Hunter's been expelled. There's been no sign of him or his vile mate Scuffer. The other two idiots are still around though but they act like they've banged their heads or something. They avoid everybody. Hunter's gang seems to be falling apart without him there to lead it.'

Toby glanced at a life support screen and noticed several of the monitor lines had peaked and were now settling back to normal. Toby frowned.

'You hear me, mate?' The lines were normal. Toby frowned. 'Jake Hunter,' he said clearly.

The lines peaked again. He was getting a response!

The door suddenly opened and Eric Kirby entered. Toby stood up, partially out of respect, but mostly out of surprise. Kirby was an old school superhero. He had once gone by the name Commander Courage—but that was a long time ago during the Second World War. To look at him you wouldn't have said Kirby was a day over fifty.

'Ah, Toby. Glad you could make it. Please sit back down, I'm not so old as to need a chair everywhere I go.'

Kirby walked over to the monitors and studied Pete's progress. The old man walked with a cane, but Toby knew that was more of a prop than a walking aid. Hidden inside the cane was a sword. It was old-fashioned, but then again so was Commander Courage.

'How's he doing?' asked Toby.

'Stable. That's about the best we can hope for right now.'

'Any sign of Emily?'

He saw Kirby hesitate. What wasn't he being told?

'We're still picking up her vitals, and she is apparently fit, well, and alert. But we still can't locate her.'

'You must have some idea where she is?'

Again the telltale pause. 'Nowhere we can get to at this present moment. But at least she is safe.'

Angry thoughts swirled through Toby's mind. Why weren't his questions being answered? After everything

# The Awakening

the four friends had done for Kirby and the Foundation, he expected to be treated better. He was beginning to understand Pete's and Lorna's frustration.

He was about to say this when something caught his attention. A cord was poking from Pete's clenched fist.

'Who's been to visit Pete?'

Kirby shook his head. 'Nobody. As you know his parents are under mild hypnosis.'

'Somebody's been here.'

He leaned across and opened Pete's hand. Inside was Lorna's necklace. So she had been here at some point today, which meant she must have left school early. But why?

Kirby was instantly alert, crossing next to Toby with a surprising turn of speed.

'It's Lorna's.'

'Are you certain?'

'Positive. But why would she leave it here? And why didn't she tell me she was coming?'

Kirby pulled out his mobile phone. Two taps on the interface and he was through to hospital security.

'This is Kirby. Send me a list of everyone who has accessed Pete Kendall's room in the last twenty-four hours.' Seconds later his phone made a mellifluous noise as the information arrived. He flicked a finger through the list. 'Only authorized personnel. If she came then she bypassed security.'

Toby heard the strain in his voice.

'Why would she do that? What's going on? What aren't you telling me?'

Kirby sighed. Toby thought the old man was terrible at bluffing . . . unless he was *very good* at it and only gave the *impression* he was terrible. Toby silenced his inner voice, life was complicated enough.

'Your sister was summoned for . . . special duty.'

'Lorna? Why her and not me?' The words were out before Toby could stop them. He knew it sounded whiny, but Hero.com was his find. His rules. Why was his sister getting preferential treatment?

'Because it's a situation that she is perfectly suited for.' He continued scanning through the security logs. 'Ah, here we are. A guest visited this afternoon, but for some reason the data is corrupt and we have no ID. Maybe that was her?' Kirby made another call on his phone. 'Security? I want a guard posted on Pete's room . . . hello? Security?' He tapped the phone. 'I was cut off.'

He dialled again—this time an ear-splitting screech played over the phone, causing him to drop it. Toby was forced to cover his ears until the shriek had died away.

'What was that?' he yelled, his ears still ringing.

'I'm being jammed. Something is very wrong.'

The door was suddenly kicked open. Toby couldn't

see anybody beyond, but he heard a distinctive *whump* of compressed air—followed by a metal cylinder rolling into the room, spewing thick smoke. Toby's eyes started to sting and tears rolled down his cheeks. He knew what the smoke was: tear gas. He coughed hard as the gas made breathing difficult.

A figure in a business suit walked into the room, a heavy-duty rifle in hand, his face obscured by a gas mask. He slammed the door shut with his foot and kept the gun trained on Kirby. The old man was on his knees wheezing asthmatically.

The figure crossed to Pete's side and systematically began yanking the leads from the life support machine.

'No! You'll kill him!' spluttered Toby. He lunged at the man, pulling his arm back. The stranger obviously didn't possess any super-strength, but he was still stronger than Toby and shook him off. Toby pressed his attack, knocking the gas mask at an angle. Through streaming eyes Toby got a look at his face. He looked like a regular middle-aged guy, with neat black hair and dressed in a business suit with a tie. If it hadn't been for the gun he wouldn't look out of place in a bank. But it was the eyes that made Toby pause. The man's eyes were completely black. Not a trace of white was left. The sight was unsettling.

Toby tasted blood and felt his two front teeth wobble. His nose and upper-lip were split as he fell.

The man continued jerking tubes from Pete's body. The last one contained a liquid super-power that was healing him. The ooze splashed across the bed.

But now the gas was clearing and Kirby had stopped coughing. Toby heard the old man draw his sword.

'Drop the gun!' he croaked.

The man didn't even give Kirby the courtesy of looking up. He levelled the rifle and shot Kirby point-blank in the chest.

Toby gasped but he was cornered and felt useless without superpowers. He pulled his phone from his jacket—but the man darted across and kicked it out of his hand. The man returned to elevate the bed so that Pete was in a sitting position. He began whispering to him.

Toby's eyes strayed to a fire extinguisher on the wall. It wasn't much of a weapon against an armed man, but he had no intention of letting the criminal get away with hurting Pete.

Very slowly, Toby reached for the extinguisher and lifted it from its hook. He stood carefully, taking a cautious step towards the man, whose back was to him. He raised the extinguisher—then slammed it down onto the man's skull with a satisfying clang.

The man collapsed, the gun clattering to the floor and his gas mask falling off. Toby kicked the gun under

# The Awakening

the bed, and felt for a pulse on Pete's neck. There was a strong one.

'Hang in there!' said Toby as he reached across for the emergency alarm.

The man grabbed Toby's ankle with a steel grip, pulling him away from the alarm. Toby spun round, face-to-face with those black eyes as the man scrambled to his feet.

'Who are you?' he screamed.

The man battled Toby aside and continued whispering to Pete. Toby was now close enough to hear that it was a string of numbers.

'Zero-one-one-zero-one-zero-one-one . . . '

Toby had no idea what they meant, but he knew it couldn't be good. 'Leave him alone!'

'Four, one, eight. Activate.'

Pete's eyes opened, and he stared vacantly ahead. The man backed away slightly.

Toby slowly stood. 'What have you done to him?'

The man looked at Toby with a puzzled expression. Then the blackness in his eyes cleared away until he looked normal. He was completely bewildered.

'W-where am I?' he gasped.

'What do you mean? You just ran in here and shot a man!' snarled Toby. The man glanced at Kirby slumped against the wall. Toby could hear the old man's bones gently snapping, and his chest wound looked smaller.

Toby was relieved that he wasn't dead and he must be slowly regenerating.

The man looked utterly horrified. 'I did that?'

Before Toby could repeat himself Pete raised his hand. An invisible telekinetic force shot from his fingers—lifting the man off his feet and smashing him forcibly through the double-glazed window.

Toby watched in horror, hearing the man scream all the way from the top floor to the ground. Toby heard shattering windows and the wail of a car alarm.

'Pete! Why did you do that? He stopped—'

Pete raised his other hand and Toby felt something grab him by the throat and pin him against the wall. His feet dangled from the floor as he clawed at the invisible force.

Pete slowly climbed out of bed, keeping one hand pointed at Toby. He reached for his glasses and looked around the room, before finally looking back at his friend.

'Pete . . . stop it. *Please* . . . '

'What happened to Emily?' said Pete in level tones.

'I don't know . . . she went missing last night.'

'Did you kill her?'

The puzzled expression on Toby's face told Pete all he needed to know. Pete stopped the telekinetic force that was holding Toby up. Toby dropped onto his bum.

# The Awakening

'What did you do that for? I've been worried sick about you.'

'Shut up!' snarled Pete. Even in his stripy pyjamas he looked menacing.

'What happened to you?'

'I had time to inwardly reflect on my life. And I realized how badly it sucked. I've finally seen that it wasn't my fault; it was the people around me making it worse, thinking they knew what was best. People like you.' Toby was hurt by the accusation. Pete's face was knotted in rage. 'You stole the best thing in my life, Hero.com, and claimed it was yours and that we had to play by your rules.'

The veins were pulsing on Pete's forehead. Toby slowly approached him.

'Pete, I'm your best friend—'

WHAM! Toby saw Pete's hand move and felt the energy blast cannoning him across the room into a cabinet full of medical supplies. He felt his skin burn, and everything sounded muffled, as if he was underwater. It was the first time he had been hit by a superpower with no form of defence.

'You're no friend of mine! You're no different from the others trying to *use* me, manipulate me. But I'll show you. I'll show you exactly what I'm capable of!'

Eric Kirby jumped athletically to his feet and walked towards Pete.

'Steady now, Pete. We know you've been through a lot, but this is the time to calm down.'

Pete fired an energy blast. Kirby raised his arm and a circular energy shield formed. The blast ricocheted upwards creating a hole through the ceiling.

'Don't patronize me!' snarled Pete. 'You of all people! Making us do your dirty work for *nothing*. Expecting us to work as *slaves* for your own causes.'

The two circled around, Kirby making sure that Toby was now behind the shield.

'You know that isn't true,' said Kirby calmly.

Pete fired another blast—this one bounced at the door, blasting it off its hinges and knocking down the four heavily armed security guards who were about to storm the room. Somewhere a siren started to wail and the sprinkler system was triggered across the hospital.

The cold water stung Toby's broken nose and split lip, but he was too full of adrenalin to be bothered.

'I know what needs to be done now,' said Pete in an oddly calm voice. 'And I know you can't stop me.'

'I wouldn't be so sure about that. You're still a little boy after all.' The taunt was just enough to irk Pete. He fired another blast of energy at Kirby.

Kirby was ready and twitched his shield at the perfect angle. The blast rebounded straight at Pete—but instead of knocking him from his feet he absorbed the

# The Awakening

energy bolt and appeared to grow bigger by a couple of inches.

Toby thought it was an optical illusion, but the fact Pete's pyjamas were suddenly two sizes too small, added to the look of horror on Kirby's face, was proof enough.

When he realized what had happened, Pete began to laugh. It wasn't a pleasant sound.

'See?' he bellowed. 'What can you possibly do to me?'

At that moment two security guards ran into the room. They made an immediate threat assessment, as they had been drilled to do in training, and pointed their guns at Pete.

'NO!' shouted Toby and Kirby at the same time.

The thunderous clamour of high-calibre bullets being shot in the room was deafening. The bullets bounced uselessly off Pete.

The impact made him grow even larger, the seams on his pyjamas starting to split. Toby didn't know what was worse, his maniacal friend or the fact that his pyjamas were about to rip off completely.

Without a second thought, Pete blasted the two guards with an energy beam. They shot out into the corridor.

'This is my time!' roared Pete. Then he looked directly at Toby. Toby gasped, whatever transformation was consuming Pete was now visible across his skin. It was bluey-green and cracked like sun-dried swamp mud.

'If I find out you killed Emily—I'll be back for you!'

The loss of blood was making Toby feel dizzy. Once again he experienced the unsettling tunnel-vision and the world seemed to flip-flap, as if everything he was seeing was projected on a large sheet of rubber.

Even more unsettling was the fact that Pete was repeating his unfounded threat. The whole déjà vu experience made Toby feel nauseous.

Pete unleashed another blast at Kirby. This one was so powerful that the old man was pitched against the wall, unconscious once again.

Then Pete roared and teleported away with a deep thunder clap.

Toby lay gasping on the floor, confused and shocked. Then the pain from his facial injuries and what felt like several broken ribs and scorched skin overwhelmed him.

He collapsed on the floor, the water from the sprinklers washing his blood away.

# Foreshock

Toby opened his eyes and saw Eric Kirby was looking at him. Toby was lying on a trolley that had been wheeled into a private office. A large plasma screen hanging on the wall showed a digital world map.

'Are you OK?' asked Kirby.

'I think so. How long have I been out?'

'About an hour.'

Toby heard a beep, and then an unsmiling matronly nurse, who was standing to his side, spoke up.

'That's a full pack. You should be feeling fighting fit.' From his arm she removed a tube that was connected to a now empty pack of raw healing superpower—the hospital's secret weapon.

Toby ran his hand over his face: his teeth didn't wobble, his lip had healed, and his burnt skin felt smooth again. A scar on his wrist itched like crazy and he wondered what Pete had done to him to cause that.

He sat on the end of the bed and gratefully accepted the cola and biscuit he was given. 'You need a sugar boost,' said the nurse by way of explanation.

'What happened to Pete?'

Kirby shrugged. 'He escaped. Enforcer units are searching for him as we speak.'

'That's not what I meant,' said Toby. He wasn't feeling in the mood for playing games. 'Why did he act like that?'

Kirby waited for the nurse to exit through a thick blast door that sealed closed behind her. Toby thought the door was an unusual level of protection. Perhaps Kirby was feeling vulnerable after Pete had beaten him.

Kirby walked across to the map and studied it. Toby noticed that there were small clocks hovering over specific locations. At first he assumed they designated the local time zones, but on closer inspection he saw they were all showing the *same* time.

'When you are chosen by the Hero Foundation, or indeed the Council of Evil, to download powers it is because we think you have the makings of a hero. Your Internet searches, your school grades, online shopping, and everything you have bought in a high street store, it's all monitored. The moment your CD or book is swiped across the till, that information is stored on a computer. And we have access to almost every computer in the world. Once you have been selected, Artificial Intelligence monitors your activities on cameras, in the street, at school, in the shops. Every email, text, and phone conversation is intercepted and analysed.'

'That sounds like a total invasion of my privacy.'

'Yes. But it's going on around you with government agencies all the time. We do it to ensure that you are worthy of the gift we are offering.'

'What's that got to do with what happened to Pete?'

Kirby turned away from the screen and looked shrewdly at Toby. 'The computer builds a psychological profile of you, and from that you are selected. Pete's profile was flagged as a potential risk, but still he got through the system. The Foundation . . . I . . . had hoped that you, Lorna, and Emily would keep him on the right track. However, it was not to be.'

'Pete's not a villain, if that's what you mean. He's just confused. His parents are splitting up, he's got a lot of issues.'

'He's not strong willed enough. His family problems are nothing; most people get through those trying times in life and without the aid of powers. I'm afraid that Pete was weak and overwhelmed by a combination of being exposed to riches and power beyond his dreams, and being bullied by Jake Hunter . . . and by you.'

Toby felt a rush of disbelief. 'Me? I didn't bully him!'

'Inadvertently you did. Bullying is not only physical.

It can be mental too. He resented your control of Hero.com. Felt it was too restrictive. This made him vulnerable to dark influences. That is your fault.'

Toby felt sick, he also felt he was being unjustly accused. He was angry that Kirby blamed him. Before he could speak, Kirby went on, 'But you have to remember, ultimately Pete chose his own path, and regardless of what you may think, it's a path of villainy.' Toby didn't know what to say. He couldn't imagine Pete as a supervillain, and he refused to believe it. Kirby continued. 'After being smothered by raw super-powers perhaps that has unbalanced him too. We're not sure what the power overdose has done or what he's capable of.'

A thousand questions stormed through Toby's head. He tried to stand, but found his legs were trembling. He needed answers.

'I need to stop him. Convince him that he's wrong. Bring back the old Pete.'

Kirby shook his head. 'Trying to convince an angry man he is wrong will only inflame the situation. This is not the time for reasoned debate.'

'You're wrong! I think I can do it. With Emily and Lorna—'

'Who are not by your side and cannot help you.' Kirby sighed.

'Whatever "special mission" you've got Lorna doing,

stop it. I need her now. We have to get our team back together and find Emily. Then the three of us can convince—'

'Alas, no. Lorna is unable to assist, and Emily is untraceable. But freeing Emily will be the key to one big problem.'

It took Toby a moment to register the sentence. 'What big problem?'

Kirby sighed again as if he didn't know where to begin. He took a remote control from his desk and pointed it at the screen. Images overlaid the map, artists' depictions of heroes from world legend.

'The Knights of the Round Table; the Greek heroes and gods: Perseus, Zeus, Hercules; the Vikings had Odin and Thor; Chu Jung and Kuan Ti of the Chinese. Figures from mythology who were really Primes. People born with superpowers. Historically, we are not a new phenomenon. In fact, history had more warrior heroes and diabolical villains than we have now. Primes are a dying breed.'

'Which is why you invented Hero.com,' said Toby, 'to create new heroes?' He knew the potted history of superheroes. 'I don't see how this is relevant to what's happening now.'

Kirby perched himself on the edge of his desk and collected his thoughts.

'What do you know about time travel?'

Toby laughed. He hadn't expected the left-field question. 'Only what I've seen on TV. And the fact that the power is not available on Hero.com. Pete and I spent an afternoon looking for it once.'

'There are several powers that are unique. Owned by individuals and never synthesized for Hero.com. They are called Core Powers and they are too powerful and destructive to be used. Time travel is one of them. Forget everything you have ever heard about it. I assure you it is all nonsense.'

'But it's possible?'

Kirby smiled. 'The power exists; it's just that everything you know about time travel is wrong. For example, right now we live in the present and the future doesn't exist. You can't travel to somewhere that doesn't exist.'

'So we're in a dead-end tunnel?'

'Yes, a tunnel that pushes forward with the present always at the head. But you can go *back* along the tunnel. That's the past.'

'So if I had the power I could go back in time, and then forward again to my present, but not into the future?'

'Precisely.'

'So I could go back and stop events from happening? I could stop wars, or even stop myself from being born?'

# Foreshock

'That is what is called a paradox. And it's impossible.'

Now Toby was confused. 'But I thought if I go back to the age of dinosaurs and step on an insect, it could change the course of history.'

'That is merely a flight of fancy, and not scientific fact. Think about how unnecessarily complex that is. If you now went back in time to give yourself the winning lottery numbers, then your future would have changed and you would not be able to go back in time to give yourself the numbers. Why would you even bother because you are now already rich? Therefore you could never have gone back in the first place. It's a paradox, it is impossible.'

Toby nodded. That made sense to him. Sort of.

Kirby continued. 'In fact the truth is somewhat more bizarre. Are you ready? The events of the *present* affect the *past* as you already know it.'

Toby's head swam. 'So, something I do today can affect events that have *already happened* hundreds of years ago?'

'So it seems. Scientists call it *retrocausality*.'

'What does that mean?'

'Google it! It means the present can affect the past just as much as the past affects the present. Scientists have conducted experiments on photons to prove it's possible.'

Toby stood up, his legs still shaking. 'Look, this is all

mind bending and fascinating, but it doesn't help with our current problems.'

'That's precisely the point. Because of what is happening now, events in the past have *already* occurred.'

'I'm more interested in my sister and my friends.'

'What is happening now is all linked to you.'

Toby sat back down. After Pete blaming him for all his woes this was too much. 'How?'

'What do you know about Lord Eon?'

'I've heard the name,' replied Toby racking his memory. 'He escaped from Diablo Island after Basilisk sprung Viral.' Diablo Island was a prison for supervillains and for heroes who had strayed. During their last big adventure Toby and his friends had tried to stop Basilisk freeing a deadly supervillain called Viral. They had failed, and that was partly what had led to the near downfall of the Hero Foundation.

'Lord Eon is a villain. He's so feared that it was the Council of Evil themselves who ensured we incarcerated him. He possesses a Core Power, time manipulation, and he is now the biggest risk the world is facing.'

'And you need me to stop him.' Kirby nodded. 'But why me?'

'Because it is fated.'

'You mean you don't know.'

Kirby laughed, a long genuine laugh. 'You're getting to know me too well. I don't know why, but I knew it had to be you. We can trace Emily's CUCI, so we know she's alive, but we cannot determine her location. She is being held outside the flow of time and space.'

Something occurred to Toby. He told Kirby about the feeling of déjà vu he'd had before Emily had disappeared and again when Pete went crazy. Kirby nodded gravely.

'The expression itself is French, meaning *already seen*. It's a sign that Eon has been meddling nearby. Think of it like ripples in a pond.'

'I don't understand why he would take Emily. For what reason?'

Kirby started pacing the room. 'Lord Eon does not see the world as we do. To him, time is not one event after another, it happens at the same moment. He perceives our world as an ever-expanding bubble—he can look in and see *everything* and *every when*. He exists like a tachyon, faster than light. He exists *in between* time. Think of it as though he lives between only one second and the next. Sometime he chooses to enter our world so he can feed off humanity's chronons.'

Toby rubbed his head. 'For the sake of argument, pretend I don't know what a chronon is.'

'It's a unit of time smaller than a Planck length.'

Toby was sorry he asked. 'I take it that's very small?'

'Very. But without it, we would be like Eon, existing in between time as we know it. Unable to ever move forwards, never mind backwards. Lord Eon has been making random appearances around the globe, abducting people and using their chronons to make himself stronger.'

'He kills them?'

'Oh no. He needs them alive. They will exist in a permanent limbo. Conscious but unable to see, hear, move . . . do anything. He has been doing this since he escaped from Diablo Island and he is growing much stronger. So strong that since taking Emily he has jumped from individuals to entire towns.'

'So why did he take Emily?'

'He's been targeting individuals to draw power from. Gather enough of them and he increases power.'

'It seems a massive coincidence if it was random.'

'Do you think she was targeted? Why would Eon do that?'

Toby shrugged, he was grasping at straws. Kirby changed the display on the screen. It showed a webcam feed that appeared to be mounted on the roof of a truck. The immediate area was swarming with people wearing colourful hazardous-material suits, complete with self-contained breathing equipment. They were all branded with the Foundation logo. Beyond stood a dense wall of cloud. Lightning zigzagged through it, and as the cloud undulated, Toby could see the occasional edge of a building.

'You are looking at a small village in Ireland. It only had a population of twenty or so, but they are all now victims of Eon. Not dead, but not really alive.'

Toby was shocked. 'Can't you send a team in there and pull the people out?'

'No. That's the real menace behind Eon's power. Once you set foot into that Time-Storm, he has you. Unless he wills it, you can't get out. Ever. Every second you once possessed is now *his*. If he has grown powerful enough to take that village, then it won't be long before he gains strength to consume the entire world. The good, the bad, and the indifferent. For Eon, this is not about power or wealth. It's about survival. This is one of the biggest dangers we have faced. The Council and the Foundation will both suffer as a consequence. We are at crisis point, Toby. This is a real end of world scenario.'

Toby felt a migraine coming on. Time was an abstract concept at best, especially if you were waiting for Pete to arrive punctually. What Kirby was proposing was really a fate worse than death. It was being held in a prison for eternity, with no possibility of escape or even movement. He could only equate it with Pete's coma, and that was awful.

'So where is Eon? Charge me up and let's get him and save Emily and the others.'

Kirby held up his hand to slow Toby's enthusiasm.

'It's not as easy as that. Remember that Eon controls time. You can't sneak up on him. You can't simply attack him and hope for the best. On this occasion brute force is not the answer. On this mission you will have to use your brain.' He flipped back to the world map on the screen and highlighted a clock. The map zoomed into an eastern region of the globe. 'This is Cambodia. See the clock?'

'Yes, but what is it. Local time?'

'Our satellites have been monitoring the globe, tracking time on earth with the use of atomic clocks, the most accurate time system there is. But we're picking up abnormalities between clocks stationed on the ground and those in orbit. They're called time dilations. The dilations show that, in those areas, time is slowing down, sometimes only by nanoseconds. That means two things. We can track Eon when he uses his power, and we can locate what we need to stop him.'

'What do you need to locate?'

'Eon is not the first Prime to be able to manipulate time although he is certainly the most powerful. In the past, when heroes were plentiful, they created a device they called the Temporal Dilator to stop these fiends. It was last used on Lord Eon. For safety, the Dilator was broken up into four pieces and hidden across the globe, protected until they were needed again. Unfortunately the knowledge of their locations was kept to a select few, and ultimately it has been lost in time.'

'That's really not helpful!'

'No, but what *is* helpful is the fact that the pieces slow time, only by a few seconds, but that is enough for our satellites to detect them.'

'I don't understand how any of this connects to me or Pete?'

'Remember events that occur *now* affect the past. The choices we make now allow the *past* to happen, but who knows what those choices are.'

'That's very cryptic.'

Kirby's face became grave. 'Since you displayed amazing skills in stopping Basilisk and co. from taking over Hero.com, you have proved to be one of the very best agents the Foundation has. It all boils down to a simple concept. We need those four pieces because Eon *must* be stopped. For the sake of the world as we know it.'

Toby expelled a long breath. 'So I need to save the world again,' he said with a trace of irony.

Kirby looked sternly at him. 'The world always needs saving.'


Pete had no destination in mind when he teleported from the hospital. He'd appeared in a small town not

49
101101
0101
00000
01101
00101
01010
1101101
0101
0101
01101
00100
0101
1101
101101
00100
0101
0101

too far away, lit by only a few flickering streetlights. He instantly recognized where he was as he'd been forced to come shopping here with his mother for second-hand clothes a few months ago. The embarrassment of that incident must have been playing on his subconscious.

He was thankful that nobody was around. His rage was subsiding, as was his increased bulk. He reasoned that his body must have absorbed the energy from the attacks on him. An interesting defence that he would have to explore at a later date.

He looked at his reflection in a dark shop window. His skin was cyan and cracked. He ran his fingers across his cheek, which felt like sandpaper. Other than his deathly appearance, he looked like the same old Pete.

But inside he felt completely different.

A confidence burned in him that he had never felt before. So did anger over the many injustices in his life. But he knew he had the power inside him to change that. He'd experienced life as a hero. Risked his life for a noble cause—and almost died because of it. And his reward? Just a pat on the back.

Blue sparks of power crackled between his fingers when he raised his hand. Strange powers flowed through his body. He had a fleeting memory of fighting Basilisk as the floating Hero Foundation plummeted to earth. His last conscious sight was a tidal wave of multi-coloured ooze swamping him. It was the volatile mix of dozens of superpowers that he and Basilisk had fought their way through.

Now he had absorbed them like a sponge, his DNA mutating and transforming to accommodate them. He didn't realize that being in a coma was his body's method of camouflaging the intense pain he would have felt during the transformation. That's why he had nearly died several times. Now the powers were part of his system. He had no idea how long they would last, but he was determined to make the most of it.

He remembered the voices that had echoed through his head during his vegetative state. Toby and Lorna whispering to him. Lorna he didn't mind, but Toby . . . thinking about his old best friend made his fists clench. Toby had dragged him into all this. Toby had prevented him from using Hero.com on his own. And to add insult to injury, Toby had started to flirt with Emily.

Pete had had a crush on Emily, and Toby had ruined that too.

Then there was the other voice, strangely familiar, whispering destructive thoughts. Unable to respond, Pete had known that his buttons were being pushed, that somebody was trying intentionally to anger him. And he remembered the final words, telling him that Toby had killed Emily; followed by Lorna's voice saying that Emily was missing. What more verification did he need? Although the look on Toby's face had indicated that he was innocent.

Pete clutched his head, trying to brush aside the conflicting voices from his memory. The last sound he remembered was a harsh screech, like electronic noise . . . then much later, the man whispering a sequence of numbers to him. He was sure that's what had roused him from his coma. He had no idea what the numbers meant, but they had had a profound effect on his subconscious.

A cold wind blew and a few flakes of snow started falling. Pete was still in his torn pyjamas. He looked back at the window, past his reflection. It was a clothing shop. Inside, mannequins were dressed in expensive street-smart clothes, exactly the kind of thing that Pete couldn't normally afford.

Things were going to change.

He blasted the plate glass apart with a short energy bolt, ignoring the piercing alarm bell, and pulled the clothes off the dummies. Within a minute he was dressed cooler than he had ever been in his life. He admired his reflection in a full-length mirror. If it hadn't been for the curious state of his skin, his new image would have been perfect.

Then he caught movement behind him.

Pete spun round, both fists clenched and pulsing

with flickering blue energy. A figure stood calmly in the shadows.

'Come any closer and I'll turn you into toast!'

'Nice. What a welcome that is.' The voice sounded familiar, but Pete was having trouble pinpointing who it was. 'After everything I've done to help you, I would have thought you'd be a little more friendly . . . *Professor.*'

The hated nickname angered Pete, and he instantly recalled the person who used it.

Jake Hunter stepped from the shadows. He was smiling.


'As you know, we've had a restructuring of how we conduct operations and deployment in the field,' said Eric Kirby as he led Toby into a white panelled room. A technician, wearing a white cotton suit, walked around them preparing futuristic looking equipment for Downloaders to use out in the field. Everything looked new.

'Since Basilisk infected the system with a virus, we have seen the danger of allowing users access to too many powers. And after what happened to Pete and . . . er . . . other Downloaders, well, you can see why we need to be careful.'

He led Toby to a table covered with equipment. Toby

reached out to take a gun-like device, but Kirby slapped his hand away.

'Like the Parser in your ear, this technology is powered by small ampoules of raw power embedded in the circuitry. This is all really next-generation gear.'

'I thought superpowers only worked on people?'

'Over the years, we have made many breakthroughs, but we were too set in our ways to implement them. But after nearly being toppled, we have had to embrace change. Our scientists have discovered a way to fuse the technology to a power, but it can only become active once a person uses it. More specifically, a super. Not a regular Joe on the street.'

'Cool!'

'Sub-zero, in fact. It relies on superconductors; supercooled circuitry that operates at fantastic speeds. Take these.' He took one of several pairs of wrap-around sunglasses. 'They resemble ordinary sunglasses, but when activated by a super it triggers the stored power, in this case X-ray vision. There's a toggle at the side for thermo-vision and night-vision.'

'That's neat, but I don't understand why that's better than just downloading the power in the first place.'

'As you know, mastering a power can be tricky. You mastered flying quite easily, but the rest of the powers, such as the energy blasts, you use them with the force of a sledgehammer because you're not aware how to fine-tune your skills.'

Toby recalled a time Pete had accidentally down-loaded X-ray vision and it had rendered him almost useless.

'The gadgets are charged with a limited amount of power, which means you are not being exposed to a full dosage, thus allowing you to use more power-gadgets in the field than you could superpowers. All with no side effects. At least none that we know about,' he added as an afterthought.

Kirby held up a thirty centimetre long black tube. 'This is clever. A tele-grenade. You twist the top and hold on—you're instantly teleported to the other side of the world, completely out of harm's way.'

'Couldn't I just use a teleportation power to do that anyway?'

'Yes, but you can throw this at an enemy and they'll disappear.'

He sensed Toby was unimpressed. He held up a backpack.

Toby pulled a face. 'What's so great about that?'

'You can put things in it.'

'I have a school bag that does that too.'

'Ah, but is your school bag a form of Tesla/Faraday cage, linked to a teleport ampoule?' Toby shook his head. 'We can fill this pack with equipment, program it

to lock onto your CUCI and teleport it to you anywhere in the world.'

Toby was impressed. 'That, I like.'

Kirby turned back to the table and indicated the rest
of the equipment. 'We must quickly go through these.
You will take a few with you on your first trip. Of
course you'll download some key powers, but this will
be your back-up. Remember, this mission relies on
stealth and intelligence, not force. You can't blast your
way through this.'

'I understand,' said Toby, although he was having
doubts. He, Pete, Lorna, and Emily had achieved
limited success as a team. Now he was an army of one.

A sudden emptiness struck him. He was alone.
Without his sister or his friends. For a moment he
longed for the innocent days before lightning had
struck the telephone pole outside their house while
they were online. That strike had led them to
Hero.com. It had caused their mother to be kidnapped
by a raving supervillain, destroyed their house, caused
jealous arguments between them all, and now torn
apart friends and family.

Perhaps Pete and Lorna had been right to ask why
they were risking everything for the Hero Foundation.

Toby closed his eyes and drew in a deep breath,
aware that Kirby was watching him carefully. Toby
hoped his sister was OK, whatever she was doing.

# Foreshock

Pete's transformation was a problem to deal with another time; in the meantime Toby hoped the Enforcers would get Pete and show him common sense.

He blanked his mind. Right now he had to stop Lord Eon from destroying the world—no small task for a kid—and in doing so find Emily. She was the one in trouble.

He opened his eyes and looked at the equipment laid on the table. He had to choose the right tools to help him find the first piece of the mysterious Temporal Dilator. Which tools would help him most in Cambodia?

He had no idea.

# Cambodia

Pete stared at Jake with contempt. He crunched across the broken plate-glass window to face his enemy. Jake Hunter, the worst bully in the school. He had made life hell for Pete over the years. From mental torment to flat out beatings, Jake's abuse had been relentless. He was the last person in the world Pete had expected to see.

And he was delighted.

On the street the two boys circled each other like boxers ready to rumble. Pete was grinning like a shark.

'I can't tell you how happy I am to see you, Jake. Your timing couldn't have been better.'

Jake regarded Pete's aggressive stance and cracked cyan skin. 'There's something different about you. Have you combed your hair on the other side or something?'

Pete wasn't listening to the taunts. This was the opportunity he had long dreamed of—armed with superpowers and confronting his bully. He'd beaten

Jake's lackeys, Knuckles and Big Tony, to a pulp when he possessed superpowers, but facing Jake was the icing on the cake.

'Do you know, there's something I've always wanted to do?'

'What's that, Professor?'

Pete smiled. Then punched Jake. Even as his hand formed a fist, Pete could sense super-strength flowing through him. In microseconds he felt his muscles firm and gain mass.

It was a perfect right-hook. Jake was lifted off his feet and sailed through the air the entire length of the street. Pete ran after him. He enjoyed watching Jake slam into the pavement and roll a dozen metres.

He reached the bully, and was surprised to see his foe stand. Jake smirked and wiped the blood from his split lip, but even as he did so the wound healed without a trace.

Pete gasped. 'You . . . you have powers?'

'Oh yeah. In fact, you might be interested to know that I have a whole new job.'

'I'm still better than you,' snarled Pete. He raised his hand, fingers extended to the heavens. Lightning crackled from them.

Jake held up his hand. 'Wait! I don't want to fight you.'

# Cambodia

'You should have thought about that before picking on me at school!' Pete extended his fingers to let rip the lightning bolt that was charging in his hand.

Jake moved faster—he raised his hand. But instead of discharging a superpower, he held a small MP3 player. His thumb was on 'play'.

An ear-piercing crackle of white noise nearly deafened Pete. He dropped to his knees, clutching his ears. It felt as though every nerve ending was on fire.

Jake stopped the MP3 and the pain dissipated with the noise.

'What was that?' shouted Pete, his ears still ringing.

'You were listening to a data algorithm. Your body translates the impulses and then communicates with the superpowers inside you.'

Pete was surprised. The Jake he knew wouldn't know what 'algorithm' meant, never mind 'data'. 'Like a virus?'

'Think of it as security, for my protection.'

'I don't understand. What do you want? Why are you here?'

'I want . . . ' Jake hesitated. The words were difficult to say. 'I want to be your friend.'

Pete was stunned by the revelation. 'My friend? I hate you. You hate me!'

'That was before all this. I've had powers about as

long as you have. Nobody else knows. I'm trusting you not to tell anybody.'

Pete was confused. 'Why did the Hero Foundation choose somebody like *you*?'

'They didn't.'

That simple reply spoke volumes. Now Pete understood where Jake was sourcing his powers. Before he could collect his thoughts, a foreign-sounding voice interrupted.

'Hold it right there, scumbags.'

Pete and Jake turned round—and they couldn't stop themselves from laughing. Two boys stood there. They looked about a year younger than Jake and Pete, and wore gloves and capes that gave them a comical appearance.

'We are the Super-Deuce-some, and we have been sent to bring you in.'

'Both of us?' asked Jake with a frown.

'Er . . . no, just him. But if you are his sidekick then you are coming too!'

Jake nodded solemnly and raised his hands. 'I'm his sidekick all right.'

Pete raised his hands too. 'Well done. Looks like you've got us.'

The two heroes exchanged glances. 'You are not going to try anything stupid, are you?'

'Nope.'

'Not at all.'

The heroes couldn't hide their disappointment. 'OK, good.'

'Is this your first time as heroes?' asked Pete.

The Super Deuce-some looked suspiciously at him. 'No. Why do you ask?' the speaker lied.

Pete remembered the first time he had downloaded powers. It was not that long ago, but already it seemed a lifetime away. He had pleaded with Toby that they have a team name and a costume. But now he saw how ridiculous that would have been.

'I remember the first time I downloaded powers. Felt like I could take on anybody.'

'We can,' said the mini-hero defiantly. He was starting to get nervous now that Jake and Pete had lowered their hands.

'Do you know the problem about Hero.com's job board? It doesn't tell you the level of threat you're tackling. I mean, take you two. Did you know you were taking on the two most powerful supervillains on the planet?'

Both heroes blanched. 'The job only mentioned you'd escaped from hospital. I thought you was some sick nutter,' said one.

Pete was thoughtful. 'Strange. That could actually be the perfect description.'

He could see the fear on their faces. Their every

movement betrayed uncertainty. Pete was enjoying the feeling of picking on them, of being more powerful than his victims.

Pete could feel the lightning power charge in his body like pins and needles. In seconds it would leap from his hands like a tidal wave.

'We're not afraid of you!'

'Then that's your mistake,' growled Pete.

Jake watched in surprise as Pete unleashed his attack. Half a dozen cars in the vicinity were tossed aside from the sheer force. The lightning ripped a half-metre trench into the road.

It was like using a sledgehammer to squash an ant.

Even Jake Hunter thought it was a brutal misuse of power.

Toby appeared with a loud bang that echoed across the jungle. He sighed, he *hated* jungles. He had been forced to trek through one in Mexico once and that had been unpleasant. This jungle felt immediately different although the humidity and the calls of monkeys and parrots seemed the same. In front of him lay a magnificent ruined city.

Toby's dad was an archaeologist, and was always enthusiastically telling his children about fabled lost civilizations across the globe. The intricate pinecone-shaped domes of the stone towers in front of Toby now were familiar, the same designs as those in the more famous Cambodian ancient city of Angkor Wat. The buildings were the size of cathedrals, yet the jungle still towered over it all, as the city seemed to have been constructed inside a massive crater, possibly created by an ancient meteorite impact. The covering foliage would have camouflaged the city from the air, which was why it was still officially 'undiscovered'.

He felt a thrill that he was looking at a discovery that his father knew nothing about. He would have to think of a way of subtly telling him about it. He pulled his touch-screen phone from his pocket and hit an icon. A bespoke program appeared. The display now resembled a radar screen, although Kirby had explained that it was a chrono-scanner that detected fluctuations in time and space. A blip flashed dead ahead: it had detected the first part of the Temporal Dilator.

Toby walked across the courtyard. Creepers had pushed through gaps between the stone flags to carpet the floor. He slowly ascended a steep staircase. Getting closer, he could see that the walls of the building were covered in weathered carvings of people and Hindu deities. His father would be ecstatic.

However, the joy of exploration soon gave way once he reached the top of the staircase. He was exhausted, sweating from *every* part of his body. He took a water-flask hanging from a utility belt with the rest of his gadgets. Kirby had insisted he take the water, and now Toby was grateful. He adjusted his belt and then moved the heavy rifle from one shoulder to the other.

Ahead was a dark portal. Toby could feel a cool breeze flow from the depths of the cavernous structure. He felt fearful. This was the first mission he had ever undertaken alone. Without his friends to watch his back, he felt vulnerable. He missed having Pete throw witty comments to relieve the sense of danger—and the thought of Pete sent a wave of remorse over him. He hoped his friend was OK and had calmed down.

Toby put on the sunglasses, and the dark passageway became completely black. Seconds later he felt a small tingle behind his ears as the superpowers in the glasses kicked in as sensors on the stems touched his skin. Then the corridor became awash with greys and greens as the night-vision activated.

He continued on, his dangling fingers tracing the intricate carvings on the wall. They felt slightly damp. The passage gently angled downwards, and Toby's trepidation increased.

Seconds before he had teleported from the Foundation HQ, Kirby had warned him to watch out for 'The Others'. It had been almost an afterthought, and Toby had wondered who 'The Others' could be.

He froze. A section of wall under his fingers had

suddenly pushed inward with a faint click. His mind raced—he was after an ancient treasure, there would surely be traps—

He spun round to see the light from the entrance fifty metres away vanish with a loud boom. With his night-vision he could see that the walls of the tunnel were slamming together in a domino effect that was heading straight for him!

Toby ran for his life. The crunch of stone hammering stone was catching up behind him. His heart felt as if it would leap from his chest, and he wished he had super-speed. But he was on his own, and he had no time to stop and download any further powers.

His trainers slid on the floor, which was becoming damper. Now he could feel the rush of air on the back of his neck as the stone blocks were hurled together with crushing force centimetres behind him.

Then he slipped. The section of floor sharply angled down and was covered in wet moss—and there was no way he could keep his balance. Toby landed hard and momentum slid him forwards. His head cracked against the tunnel wall. In the dizzying plummet he saw the tunnel crash together *centimetres* from his head—

He hit water. It was only a few centimetres deep, but it was enough to slow him down, and soak him. He rolled to a stop and became aware of the silence. He looked behind and was relieved to see he was clear of the tunnel, but unfortunately it was sealed. He would have to find another way out.

He stood, shivering and soaked. He checked his phone. Thank goodness it was waterproof. The chrono-scanner showed that the object was somewhere nearby. He also noticed that, despite the fact he had a satellite phone that was not dependent on a regular service provider, he had no signal. No chance to call for help, no way to download further powers.

Toby pulled himself together and looked around the cavern. His prize was here somewhere. What would Pete, Emily, or Lorna have done? He shook away the negative thoughts, he was on his own and he would have to deal with that.

The chamber was enormous, and covered in vivid carvings of Hindu gods. He saw on one wall detailed sequential images of a meteor falling from the sky and crashing into the jungle. It showed teams of people at the crater's edge, building a city. It was like reading a comic book, and Toby knew there would be hidden messages and meaning in what he was seeing. It would take an expert like his father to decipher it all.

The chain of images ended with a large bronze sculp-ture built into the wall. It showed a sinister figure wreathed in clouds that seemed to tower over the city. Toby suspected it was supposed to represent Lord Eon. He was being fended off by a brave sword-wielding warrior who sported four arms. The name came from the recesses of Toby's memory—Vishnu: one of the supreme gods.

Toby tore his gaze away from the mural. He wasn't here for sightseeing, and the cold dark chamber was beginning to get him worried. He turned around and jumped when he saw that Vishnu was standing right behind him!

It was a three-metre tall bronze statue of the deity. Toby's heart was pounding; he hated being alone. He would have to insist that Lorna accompany him if Kirby expected him to find the next piece of the Temporal Dilator.

In front of the statue was a dais. Rather than having a flat top, it had been carved at an angle so it looked like a stone easel. In the middle of the surface was a circular hole, no more than thirty centimetres diameter—and resting inside was a black artefact.

Toby couldn't make out any details, but he knew that must be his goal. As he carefully approached the dais, the water came over the tops of his trainers and made each step uncomfortable. The water was murky, and he couldn't see anything beneath it. He cautiously tested his weight with each step. He'd played enough games to suspect there would be a final trap.

So far so good. Toby didn't like it. His suspicions increased.

'I'm not going to fall for this,' he said aloud. His voice echoed in the cavern.

He stepped *behind* the dais. If a trap was to be triggered it would be on the fool who stood *in front*. It was awkward to reach over the sloping dais and reach inside, but he managed.

The Temporal Dilator segment was remarkably heavy, so heavy that Toby couldn't lift it with one hand. He swore to himself; why hadn't he downloaded super-strength rather than the powers he had? He never knew the right ones to download—that had always been Emily's and Lorna's speciality.

He stretched himself and reached in with both hands. Although small, the object was incredibly dense and metallic. Toby realized that it must have been crafted from the fallen meteorite he'd seen on the mural.

As soon as he moved it a millimetre, the trap triggered.

Except he hadn't been expecting *this* one.

Two stone slabs shot out inside the hole, either side of his arms. There was a smaller hole in the middle that forced his arms together with such force he felt his circulation being cut off. He was held fast in stone cuffs, stretched over the dais like a sacrificial victim.

Then he heard a grating of metal behind him. He couldn't turn his head round, but from the corner of his eyes he saw that the metal statue of Vishnu was moving!

He heard the swords swish through the air, and felt the rush of wind as the statue flexed its arms.

Without back-up, and with no way to move, Toby was *helpless*.

Jake had teleported Pete away after he had pummelled the two junior superheroes. They stood in a field not far from their home town. It was cold and snow was falling. Jake watched silently as Pete calmed down. During the attack Pete had seemed to be in a trance, completely unaware of the level of violence he was unleashing.

'Feel better now?' asked Jake.

Pete nodded. 'Those kids . . . did I . . . did I kill them?'

Jake contemplated lying and saying yes, just to see the effect it would have on Pete, but he restrained himself. He wanted to appear friendly.

'No. But your hospital is going to have to look after them extra carefully.'

Pete caught the *'your hospital'* reference. 'I don't work for the Foundation any longer.'

'Really? Then where are you going to get your powers from?'

'I don't need to download them any more.'

'Not yet you don't.' Pete looked up. Did Jake know something he didn't? Did he know how long before his new-found abilities would wear off? 'And when they do wear off, I don't think Hero.com will be welcoming you back, do you?'

Pete stared at him. The urge to barbecue his old bully with a fireball was overwhelming. Jake seemed to read his mind. 'I told you I don't want to fight. I want us to be friends. And *when* your powers start fading away, I can plug you into a whole new stream of abilities.' He was referring to Villain.net, but somehow bringing up the 'V' word didn't seem appropriate.

'Why would you do that?' Pete was rightfully suspicious.

Jake hated himself for what he said next. 'Because I'd rather work with you than work alone. We have more in common than you might think.'

Pete bit back a vitriolic reply. He was aware he might actually need a friend, or at the very least, an acquaintance.

'You've got a lot on your mind. I'll tell you what; I'll catch up with you later and see how you feel about it then. In the meantime go home, and chill out with your folks.'

Pete looked up sharply—certain that Jake knew of his family circumstances and was baiting him. But Jake had silently vanished.

# Cambodia

Pete started to trudge across the field, heading for his house. He stumbled in the snow-covered furrows before remembering that he could simply fly there.

Pete landed softly in the street. He looked at his house. Or what was left of it. It was in ruins, completely demolished after the battle to free Basilisk from his garden shed a few weeks ago.

Snow kissed the rubble. Pete could see a pile of torn comics poking from under a roofing joist. His meagre possessions had been destroyed too.

Then it hit him. He had nothing left and no idea where his parents had moved to, or even if they were still together.

Jake's words echoed in his head. He really was alone. And he had impulsively severed ties with his oldest friend and a family of superheroes who had accepted him, albeit at a price.

He shivered with the cold and pulled his hood up before walking sadly away from the life he once knew.

Toby's arms became rubbery as he triggered one of his three downloaded powers. His entire body felt like putty as he stretched three times his length. His thin arms easily slipped from the altar trap and he cart-wheeled away from trouble to the far side of the chamber. His body popped back into shape, and his mind raced for his next course of action.

The Vishnu statue whirled all four swords with perfect precision, accompanied by the sound of grating metal. The statue's head turned and targeted Toby. Then it stepped from its pedestal and stomped through the water.

Toby panicked. His night-vision was not picking up any thermals that would imply life. The statue was mechanical, and he could swear he heard the faint sounds of clockwork vibrating in the bronze body.

Toby aimed his rifle ahead. It was a prototype, designed so that Downloaders wouldn't have to load any attack powers. He levelled it at the advancing machine. The rifle had a large crystal cylinder in the middle, like the chambers on a revolver, except these were loaded with a variety of superpowers. A small dial on the stock allowed Toby to select from a number of stick-figure icons, similar to those on the Hero.com website, although nobody had bothered to explain what they represented. A wireless Internet connection ensured that he could download power-refills so the weapon would never run out of ammunition. Unless he didn't have a signal, like now.

Toby squeezed the trigger. A streamer of energy

# Cambodia

75

lashed the statue. With a crunch, the front bodywork dented and Vishnu was flung onto its back.

Toby's finger was still on the trigger when the weapon ran dry. He stared at the defeated statue.

'You weren't so bad after all!' he whooped.

Vishnu's head snapped round to follow his voice. Toby pulled the trigger again—but was greeted with a raspy sound. His trembling hands fumbled for the selector dial.

Vishnu's four swords stabbed down, lifting the statue from the water. It scuttled on them like an insect before athletically somersaulting onto two feet. The four swords clanked into position and it moved towards Toby.

Toby found the dial—the power-cylinder ratcheted round and he fired. Laser pulses shot out.

This time Vishnu was ready. The four swords were a blur as they deflected the shots. The lasers bounced from the bronze weapons, ricocheting to the floor, walls, and ceiling.

Then the gun was dry and Vishnu was upon him. All four swords thrust forwards at the same time. Toby panicked—causing his rubber-power to kick in. His entire body snapped thin, and curved like spaghetti between the blades, which had been pushed with such force they embedded into the stone behind him.

Toby super-stretched like a slinky spring across the

chamber, splashing all the way. He popped back into shape and selected another power on the gun as Vishnu extracted the swords and charged after him. The floor shook from each of the giant's footfalls.

Lightning arced from the gun and stopped the statue in its tracks. Once again the gun ran dry. Cogs still whirled inside the machine, but it didn't move. Toby slowly circumnavigated Vishnu, heading for the dais.

His feet gently swished through the water—then the statue's head turned, looking straight at him!

'Just die will you!' yelled Toby and he pulled the trigger.

Nothing happened.

He tried again and got a wheeze from the weapon. He looked closer and realized that the power-cylinders only housed three shots! Without an Internet connection it was useless.

'What? Who designed this piece of junk?'

Vishnu now turned and thundered towards him. Toby ran, feet slipping in the water. But no matter how much he zigzagged the statue followed him.

He hid behind pillars, but still Vishnu advanced. He wondered how the machine could see him—he guessed it was only clockwork and not advanced technology. Plus it would be pitch dark without his shades on . . .

# Cambodia

Dark. The answer struck Toby as he splashed across to hide behind another pillar. Vishnu turned to follow him. It was tracking noise! That's why there was water on the floor, to act as an acoustic aid!

Using his power, he stretched his arms to twice their normal length and wrapped them around a column. He lifted himself from the water, then stretched his legs across the chamber, as far as he could reach, and coiled them around another pillar.

Then he relaxed his grip. With his legs anchored, his torso whooshed across the cavern like an elastic band to join his legs!

Vishnu reached the pillar he had been behind seconds ago. The swords sheered either side of the pillar, slicing horizontally across like guillotine blades. If he had been hiding there then even his stretchy power wouldn't have saved him.

Vishnu's head slowly turned as though listening.

Silence reigned.

Toby held his breath. He knew he couldn't keep this up for ever. There was no obvious way out, and his powers would expire sooner or later.

He stretched a foot out to the dais—it was ten metres away, but he made it. He braced his other foot, then silently snapped his body across.

He was now standing on the sloping dais, with one hand gripping it so that he didn't slide off. He was directly over the hole. He stretched one thin arm through the slabs that had pinned him earlier.

His fingers stretched around the artefact like a net. He judged the hole was big enough for him to pull it through. But the weight was still an issue.

Toby tensed his rubbery arm—it pulled taut like a bungee rope. Then it snapped up, the tension yanking the Dilator with it.

Toby was forced to relinquish his grip in order to catch the heavy treasure with both hands. He slipped from the dais and splashed into the water.

Vishnu's head snapped round and the guardian advanced—at exactly the same moment that Toby's exit opened.

With a clunk of ancient machinery, the entire floor suddenly sloped down towards a central point like a funnel. As if the artefact had been a plug, now that it was removed, the water poured out through a hole that had appeared in the middle of the room. Toby slid towards it, gripping the piece of the Temporal Dilator with both hands and screaming all the way.

Vishnu crashed onto its back and slid after him.

# . . . Into the Fire

Pete wanted to vent his anger in a creative way. And the first thing he wanted more than anything else was money. As a decent law-abiding citizen, he'd never had much, so he thought things should change at the start of his new career.

He'd seen Doc Tempest rob a bank as well as clean out half the gold reserves in Fort Knox and it had looked easy. The villain would have got away with the crime too if it hadn't been for Pete and his team. All Pete had to do was pick a target. A gold reserve or jewellers would be good, but how could he convert that into actual cash? He had watched enough bad TV to know that he needed a 'fence', somebody who would pay him for the gold or jewels and then move the loot into legal businesses and accounts. The problem was he had no connections in the criminal underground. It was one thing wanting to be creatively villainous but he had no idea how to actually go about doing it.

Pete wandered the streets aimlessly, until he found he was in the wealthier suburbs of town. Emily lived around here; not that she was particularly rich, but her parents made a very good living. Thinking of her filled him with sadness. Was she really dead? How had he known she was even missing when he was unconscious? Who had told him?

Numbness overcame him: part sadness, and part hunger. He glanced around and saw that one of the big houses was in darkness and had no cars in the driveway. Without conscious thought Pete teleported inside.

The house was spacious and decorated with ultra-modern reserve. It was clear whoever lived here didn't have children as it was too tidy. The owners were not at home.

Pete headed for the kitchen and flicked a countertop TV on while he raided the fridge. The noise from the TV was welcome company. Most of the food was health-stuff—salad, grim-looking hummus, and yoghurts. At the back he found a half-full jar of peanut butter. He layered it thickly on some bread, his mind drifting back to Emily.

He missed her. He didn't miss Toby, and he was indifferent to whether he saw Lorna again. But Emily was different; he was convinced that she was more like him. He refused to believe that she was dead. He remembered the look on Toby's face; it appeared to be news to him too. And if he didn't know, then she *must* still be alive. Whoever had told Pete that Toby had killed her

had obviously done it to provoke a reaction, a violent
one like he had displayed in the hospital.

Had somebody wanted him to attack Toby and Kirby
and then break out? Then there was the mysterious
man whispering numbers to him. Who was he? Not for
the first time, Pete had the distinct impression he was
being toyed with.

He was watching the news channel. His finger
moved for the remote control and his thumb hovered
over the button to switch channels—but he froze when
he became aware of the drama unfolding at an airport
in Brazil.

He cranked up the sound. The footage was from a
helicopter hovering over a busy bay. A black Boeing
747, with a bank logo on the tail, was on the runway
well away from the terminal building. The news camera's telephoto lens zoomed in on an array of military
and police vehicles circling the aircraft.

Between the news reporter's narration and the
graphics at the bottom of the screen, Pete pieced
together that thieves in Brazil had raided a private bank
aircraft that was scheduled to transport several million
dollars. The aircraft was now grounded and the hijackers had taken the crew hostage as the police moved in.
It was a stalemate.

Perfect! The robbery had already been done. All he
had to do was teleport in, grab the cash, and get out

again in a flash. Stealing from the thieves made Pete feel like Robin Hood.

Pete took satisfaction in drinking some milk straight from the carton, something his mother had always forbidden. Then he wiped his milk moustache and set out to rob a plane.

It was a terrifying ride. Toby's stomach dropped as he plunged vertically down a tube. Then he hit a sloping floor and was carried along with the water. The tunnel violently twisted and turned, and Toby clung on to the heavy artefact as rank-tasting water splashed into his mouth. Century-old tree roots whipped at his face, tearing off the night-vision shades.

He completed the rest of the ride in utter darkness, which was even scarier. Then he saw a light ahead. It developed into a circular opening that was camouflaged by dangling creepers and tree roots, which he pushed through at speed before he dropped under water.

Toby kicked wildly. The Temporal Dilator was dragging him down and there was no way he could swim with it. He flailed frantically—then he landed on the bottom bum-first. He kicked out, intending a valiant swim for the surface—

But instead he found himself standing in a pool of

water that came to his waist. He gulped in the air, relieved to be alive. Then he took stock of his surroundings.

The tunnel had deposited him in a clearing somewhere in the middle of the jungle. The pond he was standing in wasn't particularly big and he waded ashore without a problem, slimy weed sticking to his clothes.

He sat down, exhausted, and pulled out his phone. One tap of the built-in teleport power and he would return to the Foundation.

The screen was a mess. The surface was unblemished, once he wiped the pond mud from it, but the actual display was nothing more than fragments of glitched data. Toby groaned—it wasn't waterproof after all, merely splash resistant.

Then it hit him: he had no way of getting back. His only lifeline had shorted and he had no powers to fly or teleport. He was stuck.

'Brilliant!' he shouted in frustration. 'Now what do I do?'

'You could always give me the Dilator,' said a voice from behind.

Toby whirled round, instantly on his feet, the artefact cradled in both hands. An attractive Japanese-looking girl with an American accent was standing behind him. She couldn't be more than eighteen and was dressed casually; too casually for the jungle. She had to be a Downloader.

'Who are you?'

'Oh . . . you could say I'm a collector of the exotic.' She smiled sweetly.

'Can you get me out of here?'

'That depends on how reasonable you're going to be.'

Toby detected the threat in her voice. Then he recalled Kirby's parting words about watching out for 'the others'. He guessed she was one of them. But was she another sent by the Foundation on the same quest? Or had she been sent by Villain.net? Which side was she on?

'Listen . . .'

'Jen,' she said with a polite nod.

'Jen . . . I don't know what's going on here. Really I don't.'

She looked at him quizzically, and then laughed. 'No way! Seriously?' Toby shrugged. 'Wow, I thought they were kidding when they said you could be naive. When you've been a Downloader as long as I have you tend not to believe the rumours.'

Toby was confused, a dozen questions popping in his mind. He scanned the clearing, but they seemed to be alone.

'How long have you been a Downloader?' he asked

nervously, trying to buy time so he could think of an escape plan.

'Since it used to be dial-up!' She stuck her finger down her throat, emphasizing how sick that was. 'It was so slow we used to call it "an hour a power". Anyway, shrimp, enough yapping. Give me the Dilator.'

She was mocking him, and that irked him. 'Not on a first date. And I still don't know who you are.'

Jen scowled, her fluffy persona dropping. 'I'm the girl who is stopping you, and getting that piece for my bosses. They have a lot of questions they want to ask you too which makes me feel bad if I have to kick your butt to bring you in.'

'Your bosses?'

She started circling him, eyeing him now as an opponent she must fight. 'Quit stalling, shrimp. This jungle is crawling with Agents like me, all looking for you. You see, it's like a treasure hunt. We want what you want. We know all about you, Toby Wilkinson.'

Toby was startled that she used his name. This made her smile.

'We know what you've done, and we know how you think. I've got much better tricks than you. I know you got the first piece from those jokers in Germany, kudos to you. But that one is mine.'

Toby couldn't help but blurt it out: 'First piece?'

Jen blinked in surprised. 'Dude, you *really* don't

know what's going on? Aw, I almost feel sorry for you. *Almost.*'

Toby raised his rifle. It was out of ammo but if he could get a signal and download another charge—

Jen held up her hand, as if to say: 'Stop'. Then the air shimmered and Toby felt a wave of pressure slam into him. It carried him metres across the clearing, ripping up trees in a flow of rippling air. He was surprised to see he was still clutching the artefact when he landed. He knew if he hadn't downloaded a shield power then he probably would have been splattered like a bug.

Jen advanced towards him, a fierce expression marring her face. 'Last chance, shrimp.'

Sparks flickered from his gun. Toby had nothing to attack her with. He would have to make the most of his powers to evade her. He stood up on shaky legs and managed a defiant smile.

'Is that all you've got? I'm not going to waste my time talking to you.'

He stretched his leg out—and fell flat on his face at the edge of the pond!

His rubber-power had expired. And if that had gone so had *all* his powers, including his shield. If she hit him again, he would die.

'I've had enough of this,' said Jen, holding her hand up. 'You realize the TV shows I've missed waiting in this hellhole for you to turn up?'

# . . . Into the Fire

She had taken a deep breath to rant some more, when the pond next to her exploded and the mechanical Vishnu somersaulted out. A flailing sword cut her arm as the giant flipped overhead. The ground shook when the guardian landed, water pouring from its dented bronze flanks.

Its head turned uncertainly as it sensed two targets. Toby took the chance and ran.

He fled into the jungle, branches and vines whipping him. He heard a scream and more thunderous footsteps behind him as Jen and Vishnu fought. Toby ran as fast as he could, leaping over fallen logs and boulders. A difficult task with a heavy weight cradled in his arms.

Then he heard an explosion, and assumed that Jen had dealt with the mechanical monster. His suspicions were confirmed moments later when the jungle behind him started to tear apart under an immense pressure wave.

As thick tree trunks shattered into splinters behind him, Toby threw himself into a ditch. The pressure wave passed overhead. He was unharmed. That was something.

He lay still, his ears throbbing from the change in pressure. Then he heard branches cracking and leaves rustling. Jen was approaching. His heart beat faster. He knew he should run, but he couldn't muster the strength.

Jen appeared at the top of the ditch. 'There you are, shrimp!' she exclaimed as if they were playing a game.

Her next words were lost as a bolt of energy burst into her from the sky. She shrieked and fell.

Seconds later a disc-shaped aircraft dropped vertically and hovered over him. It was a smaller version of the circular craft he had seen the Council of Evil use in France, but this one had the legend Hyper Energy Research Organization branded on the side.

The craft gently touched down in the clearing Jen had made and the ramp opened up. Eric Kirby waved him over.

'Come, my boy! Are you hurt?'

Toby shook his head. Then ran gratefully aboard.

'Do you have the piece of the Dilator?' asked Kirby urgently. Toby had the impression that Kirby would push him out if he said no.

Toby handed it to him. For the first time he got a good look at it. It looked like a squid—an egg-shaped head with thin twisting limbs branching off in one direction. It was made from meteor iron and carved with amazing precision. The limbs were covered in detailed lines and channels like an ancient circuit board.

Kirby placed it in a compartment that sealed with a hiss. Then he turned back to Toby.

'Good job. Now, let's get you cleaned up and on to the next task.'

Toby leaned back in the seat and closed his eyes. He was so tired he fell instantly asleep.

Pete appeared at the edge of Santos Dumont Airport in Rio de Janeiro. Nobody seemed to notice that he had arrived. He quickly studied his surroundings. The runways lay north-to-south. The black Boeing 747 was isolated at the north end. Beyond, the Rio Niterói Bridge spanned the harbour that opened up behind him. Through the smog to the south-west, Pete could make out the thirty-eight metre tall iconic statue of Christ the Redeemer, with its outstretched arms, keeping a watchful eye on the city from atop Corcovado Mountain.

He turned his attention back to the aircraft. All seemed quiet. The police line kept a respectful distance away. Pete's heart hammered in his chest. He was experiencing a mix of the thrill at the thought of his impending wealth and nervousness at his first criminal activity. All he had to do was teleport into the aircraft and then teleport out with the cash.

That was when he discovered the flaws in his plan.

The teleport superpower was exceptionally useful, but it took more effort to teleport greater distances. At home he could have zipped effortlessly around town, but he realized he had exhausted it by teleporting to South America. The power needed time to 'recharge'. That meant that even if he could teleport into the plane, he couldn't get back out again straight away. And in that time the police might storm the aircraft and the money could be beyond his reach.

The second flaw was that he had no idea *what* super-powers he had absorbed. He was more than aware of the Foundation's collection of 'useless' powers, having fallen victim to downloading several in the past. He hoped that when it came to a fight he wouldn't blow bubbles from his fingertips or change the colour of his attacker's hair with a flick of the wrist. He'd fallen foul of the bubbles before, and he had seen the hairdressing power online. That had baffled him and Toby for weeks.

Pete took a deep breath and calmed himself. He knew he was panicking, trying to talk himself out of what had to be done. His conscience sounded like Toby, and that infuriated him. He was his own boss now. He was doing this for *himself*. He would perform a quick smash and grab.

Without further hesitation, Pete flew across the runway at full speed.

A murmur ran through the police line as they saw a black object streak across the runway and smash into the aircraft's hold. At first they thought somebody had fired a missile—but there was no explosion. The police chief smiled knowingly and turned to his companions:

'Grupo de Operações Especiais!' He breathed a sigh of relief. At last, GOE, the police's elite Special Forces Unit, was moving into action. That would prevent a bloodbath.

Chaos erupted inside the aircraft. Pete punctured the fuselage like a cannonball. He tore through two pallets of neatly wrapped currency that exploded into the air, falling like paper snow. He came to a sudden halt in front of a startled hijacker.

'It's another kid!' the hijacker yelled.

Pete raised his hand and a blast of lightning propelled the hijacker against the wall. He slumped unconscious.

The entire fuselage had been cleared of the seats and compartments usually found in a 747. This plane was owned by a bank and specifically designed to ferry its valuable cargo around the world. Four other hijackers stared at Pete, bringing their Uzi sub-machine-guns to bear.

A fifth man stood over the crew, who were bound and gagged in the centre of the plane. Amongst them was a kid wearing thick glasses.

'Kill him!' roared the leader.

The men with the Uzis hesitated. 'He's only a boy.'

The leader grabbed a machine-gun and sprayed Pete with the full ferocity of six hundred rounds per minute.

Gun smoke filled the air as Pete was knocked to the floor, each bullet feeling like a punch to the ribs. The leader didn't stop firing until the weapon was empty. He thrust it back into his henchman's hand.

'Disobey me again and *you* will be the first hostage to be executed! Throw the body outside!'

Two of the thugs crossed to Pete. He was sprawled on the floor, but there was no blood. Odder still, Pete appeared to have grown! Pete climbed to his feet and the thugs got their first proper look at him.

His cracked skin seemed bluer than ever. Muscles rippled under his clothing, and he was now the same size as the men.

'Hit me again, I dare you!' he snarled.

The two men opened fire in unison. Pete staggered from the onslaught, but he still increased in size.

The men stopped, completely baffled.

Pete laughed. 'I'm absorbing the energy from your bullets! Every time you hit me, I'm going to get bigger and stronger!'

Pete punched one guy so hard he slammed into another pallet of cash. The other gunman tried to reload—but Pete blasted him square in the chest. It was so intense that the man's clothing caught fire, as did the pallet of money next to him. The man rolled in agony, dousing the flames.

The smoke detector in the aircraft started to wail and a dense cloud of $CO_2$ poured in from the sprinkler system to extinguish the flames.

The lead hijacker started to yell and his remaining two gunmen fired blindly at Pete. A few shots clipped his arm, but did nothing more than transfer their energy to him. He was feeling great!

He slammed both fists together and aimed into the dense $CO_2$ cloud where he could see the flicker of muzzle flashes. The energy that leapt from his fists was so bright that it left an after-image on his retinas. He couldn't see what happened to the gunmen, but they were thrown outside as the rear cargo ramp was blown from its hydraulic hinges.

The cloud of gas cleared through the door—and Pete could see the lead hijacker staring at him in awe. The man's gaze then snapped to the bound crew and he snatched a grenade from his belt and yanked the pin out with his teeth—holding it threateningly above the captives.

'One move and I'll—'

Pete moved. It was instinctive. He had no idea what would happen.

He blew at the hijacker—a mist gushed from his

mouth and covered the thief. The man just had time to move and Pete saw the grenade's trigger spring off. It seemed to be the only sound as it hit the floor.

Pete and the captives braced themselves for the explosion—instead the mist solidified into a transparent bubble that encapsulated the thief. The grenade detonated within the bubble with a muffled bang. The transparent walls took the force of the impact, but the hijacker inside didn't. Everybody looked away from the grisly sight.

Pete tore the ropes from the captives. They looked at him fearfully.

'Run!' he bellowed.

Without hesitation, they ran from the aircraft. Pete turned back to the money. Some of it had burned, but there was still plenty to take; millions in fact. Not that he could take it all, but all he had to do was fill his pockets before the police swarmed the aircraft. His bones cracked as he shrank back to normal size; the stored energy from the bullet strikes had dissipated.

'Thanks for that! You were terrific!'

Pete spun round to see the kid had remained behind. He was thumbing his mobile phone.

'I said get out of here!'

'It's OK. I can handle it from here,' said the boy, distracted as he stared at his mobile; adjusting his glasses.

'What a bad time for my powers to go! I'm an idiot! I should have set my stopwatch running.'

It dawned on Pete who this kid was. He snatched the phone from the boy's hand and stared at the screen. It said Hero.com.

'No you don't,' said Pete as he crushed it in his hand.

The boy paled. 'You're not a hero are you?' He looked at the money in astonishment. 'You're stealing from the hijackers!'

Pete began stuffing money in his jacket, in his pockets, waistband, anywhere he could put it. The boy grabbed his arm.

'I can't let you do that!' he squeaked. 'It's not right.'

'Beat it!' Pete punched the kid. He didn't want to hurt him; after all, he was un-powered. The kid still flew from the aircraft, rolling end-over-end on the runway. Pete felt a little guilty; the kid reminded him of his more innocent self and the fall must have hurt.

Then he heard the sound of approaching vehicles. The police were ready to storm the plane. He stuffed his jacket full of cash and zipped it up to his neck. An armoured car screeched to a halt under the Boeing's tail. The police chief led his men out and a dozen automatic rifles pointed at him.

'Freeze!' screamed the cop.

Pete accelerated straight up. He broke through the roof of the aircraft and hung several feet in the air to get his bearings. Loose banknotes trickled down the legs of his combat trousers.

Below, the GOE team spread out and gazed up at him in wonder. He saw rifles raised . . . then they were hesitantly lowered.

*They're afraid of me*, thought Pete with some satisfaction. It took him a moment to register the thumping sound of helicopter blades behind him. A mean-looking Helibrás AS 565 AB Panther military helicopter was pointing straight at him, weapon pods bristling.

Pete shot off towards the mountains to the south. Once he cleared the airport he skimmed low over the bay, the water cutting a V-wake from the pressure. The helicopter turned to follow.

Pete weaved between the pleasure craft dotted around the bay. Sunbathers on deck didn't quite comprehend what they were seeing as he zipped past, money streaming from his trousers. The helicopter roared close behind.

Ahead, Pete saw an island with a small peak on the right and a larger peak of quartz and granite on the left—the famous Sugar Loaf Mountain. He zoomed towards the larger peak, hoping that he could ambush his pursuers at the mountain. He gained altitude, forcing the chopper to follow him in a steep climb.

The Panther's pilot tracked Pete with his head-up display. He had stopped meandering, which made him an easier target. A small crosshair moved over him, and the pilot heard a tone indicating that the missile had locked on. He fired.

The heat-seeking missile arced through the clear blue sky and hit Pete in the back.

Pete felt as if he'd been run over by a car. Despite his powers it was incredibly painful, and he was thrown aside. He felt his body crack as it absorbed the explosion and grew. His clothing stretched, seams threatening to burst—and then they did, spilling a cloud of money.

Then his flying powers packed in.

As he plummeted to earth, he could only assume that his absorption power must negate the flying one. What a way to discover that!

His arms and legs flailed wildly and he hoped that his superpowers would cushion the fall. But since he was still aching from the missile impact, he doubted he would survive.

Then he slammed onto the pulley wheels of a large glass-panelled cable car that stretched up to the peak of Sugar Loaf Mountain. The entire car bounced on its cables. The sixty-two tourists packed inside screamed as the vehicle ground to a halt and swung like a pendulum.

Pete rolled off the gear wheels and fell two metres onto the roof of the cable car, prompting further screams from inside. He peeked over the edge. It was a dizzying drop to the island. Without a flying power to help him, Pete felt a wave of vertigo and he gripped the steel arms that suspended the car.

The Panther helicopter hovered alongside. He knew they would never risk shooting him in case they hurt the innocent tourists. Pete had the advantage. He raised one hand to shoot—

Then the world seemed to ripple, as if he was watching it all through the surface of a pond. It was an unsettling effect that caused him to grip the steel arm again with both hands.

That's when he noticed that the chopper was frozen in the air, rotors stationary. In fact the cable car itself was immobile mid-swing, but Pete could move freely.

'What's happening?' he said to himself. His voice sounded muffled, as though he was speaking in thick fog.

'You are out of time,' said a disembodied voice. It sounded like a dry whisper.

Pete looked around. He couldn't see anybody. 'Who are you?'

The voice came again; it seemed to come from *everywhere*. 'My name is Lord Eon, and I wanted to take a moment of your time . . . '

# Another Piece

'I want to speak to Lorna.'

'I'm afraid that's impossible at the moment.'

Eric Kirby sat back in the chair; his expression indicated that conversation was over. Across the table, Toby wasn't going to be ignored so readily.

'Why not?'

'Because she is . . . deep *undercover*.'

Toby crossed his arms. 'Well, I'm not going to help you again until I can speak to her.'

Kirby slammed his fist on the desk and jumped to his feet, his face crimson with anger.

'Dammit, son! This is no time to act like a *child*! Lorna is indisposed, and your friend Emily? Her life is in the balance! So stop complaining!'

Toby was taken aback by the uncharacteristic display of anger. The mention of Emily had made him feel selfish.

'I'm sorry,' he mumbled. 'This whole thing with Pete has me on edge. And I'm not used to going out there alone. I didn't feel prepared.'

Kirby's expression softened and he sat back down.

Toby pressed on. 'But you are not telling me the full situation. The girl who attacked me; she was a Downloader. She said others were looking for me. And she also mentioned we have a piece of the Temporal Dilator already. The object that we recovered in Germany.'

Kirby hesitated. Toby instantly suspected that the old man was deliberating which bits of truth to tell him. Still, something was better than nothing.

'Yes. The Temporal Dilator section you retrieved was en route from a museum in Berlin. I apologize, but it didn't seem relevant to tell you, as we are only interested in the parts we *don't* yet have. As for the girl and the people she mentioned who were hunting you, I did warn you to keep an eye out. They are Downloaders recruited by Villain.net to retrieve the artefact.'

'Why? I thought we were all in this together?'

'Why? Why do you think? Whichever side has mastery of time will be the winning side.'

'But I thought this was about capturing Lord Eon and putting him back behind bars on Diablo Island.'

'Yes, yes, of course it is. But don't be naive, boy.' Toby smarted at his harsh tone. 'Of course Lord Eon was being experimented upon when he was a prisoner. Any attempt to unlock his powers was done for a worthwhile cause. The Temporal Dilator was originally created to subdue him in the past so it must be linked to his powers. We don't know how. However, it is something we can use not only to stop him, but *control* him.'

'And you promise that once we get this device he will be locked up again, and we'll get Emily back from his clutches?'

'You have my solemn promise.'

Toby nodded thoughtfully. 'OK. Before I go after the next piece I need to give my parents some excuse as to where I am, and I need sleep.'

'Your parents have been given a cover story so don't fret about that. As for sleep, you have one hour before you depart on the next stage of the quest.'

Toby sighed. He was feeling exhausted already. 'Where to this time?'

Kirby called up the plasma wall map. More time codes were blinking on the screen. Toby noticed one was pulsing red in Brazil.

He pointed to it. 'What's that?'

'A major time disruption. Eon's handiwork. We're dealing with it. But what concerns you is right here.' The map zoomed into Greece. 'Home of arguably the greatest supers who ever lived.'

Toby stared at the map, then looked back at Kirby.

'This time I'm going to need some real equipment,

not the *rubbish* stuff you sent me out with last time. It wasn't even waterproof.'

Kirby laughed.

'It's not water you need to worry about *this* time.'

Another blip of the map started to flash red. They both watched as a message flashed on the screen: TIME DILATION DETECTED. The map zoomed to the south-western coast of Africa, in Namibia.

'Is that Lord Eon again?'

Kirby looked solemn. 'Yes. He is rapidly extending his reach. We don't have much time left.'

Pete stared at the piles of cash stacked neatly on the table. It was almost fifty grand. From the size of the pile he estimated that an additional two hundred thousand must have slipped from his clothes over Rio de Janeiro. But the pile in front of him represented more wealth than he had owned in his entire life. It felt great.

A gentle breeze flowed in at the open balcony doors and he crossed over and gazed outside. He was in the penthouse suite that offered stunning views across a dark city . . . wherever it was.

His muscles ached and his body was badly bruised, but nothing seemed broken except his glasses. Even with all the superpowers in the world he still had to wear them. That was almost as depressing as having no friends.

He threw his damaged spectacles on the bedside table and jumped on the spacious super-king-sized bed. It was the most comfortable thing in the world. He stared at the ceiling and thought what fun he could have with all that money. Unfortunately everything he could think of involved his old mates.

He felt a pang of loneliness. He stared hard at the ceiling, trying to put them out of his mind. He concentrated on the blurred sprinkler—and was surprised when it snapped sharply into focus.

Pete jumped off the bed in surprise. The entire room was in focus! He ran to the window and could pick out the traffic below in detail he had never experienced before. He could see perfectly without his glasses! Somehow his superpowers had cured his shortsightedness. He whooped with delight then collapsed back on the bed, elated and thoroughly exhausted.

His mind replayed those last few hours atop the cable car. The invisible Lord Eon had offered Pete a simple proposition—help him in a task or die where he stood.

Eon could see potential futures and had telepathically shown Pete the possible fates that lay ahead. If he shot the helicopter down it would spin out of control into the cable car, and even with all his superpowers, he would die in the fall. If he didn't shoot it down, a sniper would pick him off. The shot wouldn't kill him, but his expanding mass as he absorbed the bullet would cause the cable car to snap from the wire—with the same grisly result.

Pete had accepted the job without asking what it was. Then he had abruptly found himself in this hotel room, which had been pre-paid for and booked under the name Don Lore, whoever he was. All Pete knew was that it was great to live Don's life!

All he had to do was stay in the luxury room and wait to be 'activated'. He had access to hundreds of TV channels, but the urge to spend the loot on the table and the burning desire to explore his superpowers meant he was rapidly growing bored. For now, though, he felt exhausted, and within minutes he was in a deep sleep.

It was morning when he was rudely awoken with the telepathic knowledge of *exactly* what he needed to do. He sat upright, as if a foghorn had sounded under his pillow. Grabbing his clothes, he quickly cleaned his teeth before leaping off the penthouse balcony . . .

Toby appeared on a hillside overlooking a picturesque turquoise sea. Several miles in the distance he saw a town of spotless white houses built along the steep cliff. Blue domes occasionally broke the white, but it all seemed very natural and still—and very traditional.

Even though it was winter, the weather was pleasant. He walked through the dry grass towards a set of ancient ruins, a rocky memory of what once stood there.

He recalled Kirby's briefing before he left. The time fluctuations were coming from underground. His new phone was programmed with the exact GPS coordinates. All he had to do was follow the on-screen map then break through the ground to retrieve the third piece of the Temporal Dilator. This mission seemed easy enough.

After a few minutes slowly walking through the knee-high ruins, the GPS bleeped, indicating he was on target. He had a backpack full of equipment, plus space enough to carry the heavy artefact. The repaired rifle was slung over his shoulder. The only apparent downside to the plan was Kirby's revelation that, after analysing the last piece Toby had brought in, he had found that the mysterious properties that surrounded the artefact negated teleportation. Toby remembered that Lorna had had the same problem trying to recover the piece of the Temporal Dilator in Germany. He would have to be picked up after he sent a video-message back to Kirby.

He ran a hand across the dry earth. It seemed solid

enough. Kirby had told him that the ruins were Minoan, one of the ancient Greek civilizations. The name rang a bell, but he couldn't think why.

He looked around to check he was alone. He didn't need strangers investigating why he was snooping around, and he certainly didn't need any supervillains tracking him down.

He pulled a small pistol-like object from his utility belt and pressed it into the earth. He squeezed the trigger and the device made a dull thumping sound. Toby examined a small screen on the back of the 'pistol'. It had fired a sound wave through the ground, and would pick up any reflected signals—sonar through the ground.

The screen showed that there was an open chamber fifteen metres underground. Satisfied, he selected an extra power from his phone. He had downloaded some basics, but had insisted he needed access to POD on standby. Kirby had reluctantly agreed.

Within seconds the superpower downloaded and the screen pulsed as the power was transferred to him. It was a much better, and quicker, system than the old probing tentacle from the first generation of Hero.com.

Toby prepared himself, and then focused on his new power. Instantly his body turned to a fine dust that cascaded through the earth. It was an unusual feeling to be poured through the dirt. He was fully conscious and could feel when his body encountered any rocks. In that case he would simply flow around them.

Toby trickled through a crack in the ceiling and reconstituted on the floor of the sunken chamber. It was like sand being poured into a Toby-shaped mould.

He looked around his new environment and was immediately aware that somebody had been here before him. Chemical light sticks, fifteen centimetre tubes that activate when shaken, lay on the floor emitting an eerie green luminescence. They could burn for hours, unlike the small glow sticks he and his sister used to buy at the fair.

Toby gripped his rifle. In the few hours he had been back at the Foundation they had modified it to hold six attack powers. He could see the hasty welding, and in one place, liberal use of gaffer tape to hold the thing together. He sighed, his life was dependent on dodgy DIY.

He proceeded out of the chamber, and into a perfectly square corridor. He reached a T-junction and his heart sank as he looked left and right. He'd had enough of tunnels in Cambodia. He saw a chem-light was still burning far down the left-hand tunnel that sloped steeply down.

He followed the corridor to the marker—it was another junction, this one a crossroads. In every direction the corridor turned so he couldn't see beyond. The place was like a labyrinth.

He concentrated hard, and noticed the faint reflection of green light on one of the corner walls. Whoever was ahead of him had gone down the right-hand passageway and lit a flare around the corner.

The passage turned and a series of carved steps led downwards. At the bottom was another marker. The steps were beautifully preserved and he caught carvings of ancient Greek life on them. His father would love this place too.

For half an hour Toby followed the line of chemlights past junction after junction. Whoever had left them had known there was a maze here and had wanted to ensure they could get out. It obviously wasn't cavers—which only left one alternative. The villains were ahead on this one.

Toby thought he must be down at least to sea level, if not lower. The air was warm and stuffy, and he was starting to sweat heavily.

He turned yet another corner—then quickly ducked back for cover. There was somebody ahead!

The corridor opened up into a huge chamber: the ceiling was over ten metres high. Four pillars stood in the centre of the chamber, carved into gigantic men holding the ceiling aloft. Toby risked another peek—they were men with bulls' heads. Minotaurs!

# Another Piece

Now it came to him why Minoan sounded familiar. It was the ancient civilization of King Minos who constructed an elaborate labyrinth under the city to contain the Minotaur. As far as Toby could remember, that was supposed to be in Crete, which lay to the south of his current location. He supposed it wasn't beyond reason there were multiple labyrinths.

The figure standing in the room was a girl, and Toby had to suppress a startled gasp when he recognized Jen. She was standing motionless. Several metres in front of her lay a massive golden statue of a bull's head the size of a car. Its eyes blazed blood red, filling the room with a malevolent glow and an intense heat.

Toby waited for Jen to move. But she didn't. He started to get frustrated. He ensured the rifle was ready to fire and stepped out.

'Don't move or I'll shoot you.'

'Toby?' Jen didn't move her body, but she craned her neck around. 'Hey, how's it going, shrimp?' She tried to sound casual, but there was a tremor in her voice.

Toby was becoming suspicious. His eyes scanned the room for anything amiss.

'Turn round slowly.'

'Ah, that's the problem—I can't. And if you take another step, neither will you.'

Toby's foot froze mid-step. He glanced at the floor. It was covered in perfectly aligned hexagonal porcelain tiles.

'Are they booby-trapped?'

'Uh-huh. If I take one step forward we'll both be pancakes.'

Toby looked up. The section of roof the Minotaurs held was substantially lower than the ceiling around the edge. In the chemical light he could make out hinges in the arms of the silent guardians. Jen must have spotted them too. They would slam the ceiling down on any unsuspecting treasure hunter.

Now he was paying attention, he could see there was something held in the mouth of the golden Minotaur head, but the jaw concealed what it was.

'Are you sure you triggered the trap?' he asked.

'Totally. The tile moved down a few inches and I heard a clunk. I'm stuck.'

Toby grinned. He shouldered the rifle. This would be easy. He rose in the air and gently glided over the trick floor to the golden head. The head was dipped, as if bowing. This close he could see that this piece of the Temporal Dilator looked *exactly* like the one he already had.

'What's it like?' asked Jen. From her vantage point she couldn't see it clearly.

'Wait a minute.' He reached for it.

# Another Piece

Jen watched him with panicked eyes. 'What are you doing?'

'What does it look like? I'm getting the artefact and getting out of here.'

'If you touch that I'll move my foot and that roof will come smashing down.'

'Killing us both. You don't look like the suicidal type. I'll take the chance.'

He reached for the artefact again—

'Wait!' she yelped. The pressure was really getting to her. 'It might be booby-trapped too!'

Toby hesitated. He wished he had got some new shades; they had X-ray vision as well as night-vision. He could have seen if there were any traps. Stupid! He would bring some next time.

'In that case I better grab it quickly and fly out of here.' He looked at the roof. 'And I reckon I can make it from here to the door before that falls.' He would have to fly at full speed, but it looked possible. He hoped he wouldn't have to.

'Look, I'll do you a deal. You help me out of here and we can argue over the artefact above ground.'

Despite the tension, Toby laughed. 'Why would I do that? You were quite happy to try and rip me apart in the jungle.'

'Who left who lying injured on the floor? Who left who battling a giant mechanical freak?' Toby knew she had a point. 'Look, Toby, I know deep inside that you're a good guy. You wouldn't leave me here to die.'

Toby looked away. She was right. Even if she was a villain, he couldn't let her die. And she was cute . . . he shook away *that* thought. She was looking at him with pleading eyes.

He sighed deeply. 'OK, this is how we're doing this. I'm going to put the artefact in my backpack. Then I'll fly across at full speed, pick you up and we'll land in the corridor. Then you're going to give me twenty minutes to get out before you follow. Do we have a deal?'

Jen weighed up the various options she had. She had none.

'Deal.'

Toby licked his lips and reached for the artefact.

'Wait!'

He jumped, startled. He turned angrily to her. 'What?'

'Are you sure you can pick me up?'

Toby felt a flush of pride. 'Of course I can. I'm strong.'

'Super-strong? Or . . . ?'

'Do you want saving or not?' he snapped irritably.

Jen held up her hands to indicate the argument was over. Toby turned back to the artefact. It was held in the bull's jaws, with either end poking from the mouth.

# Another Piece

As far as he could tell there were no wires or mechanisms attached to it.

He pulled the artefact. It wouldn't budge.

'Be careful, Toby.'

Toby had his back to Jen, but he pulled a face anyway, mentally telling her to shut up. He tried again—it was held fast in the jaws. He placed both feet on one side of the head, gripped the artefact with both hands, and pulled hard. He groaned with effort— and the artefact began to haltingly slide out.

'You're doing it!' shouted Jen enthusiastically.

Toby pulled harder—and the artefact came loose. The Minotaur's jaws snapped shut. He was sweating from the effort.

'Great! Now get me out of here!' demanded Jen.

The artefact looked identical to the last one and was equally heavy. He placed it in his backpack, and secured the weight. He realized he was bobbing dangerously low over the floor.

'The weight is dragging me down.'

Jen was furious. 'You promised!'

'I'll drop the pack in the corridor and come back for you.'

'Toby!' There were tears in her eyes. 'Please!'

'I promise! If I fly you out now we'll both crash . . .'

He trailed off. There was a cracking noise behind him like ice breaking, or—

HERO.CØM

'Toby, the wall!'

Cracks crisscrossed the wall around the Minotaur's head. A fierce red light glowed behind. Toby realized why it was so warm.

'Magma? How deep are we?'

'Don't you ever read up where you're going on a mission? Santorini is an *active* volcano! It did one of the biggest volcanic explosions on the planet in the last thousand years!'

'Oh hell!'

CRUMP! The wall chose that moment to give way and searing hot magma oozed through.

Toby sped across the chamber. He tackled Jen around the waist, but as he feared they both sharply dipped to the floor. They were moving so fast that they rolled across the tiles, triggering more pressure pads.

But one was enough. The moment Jen's foot left the pad an ancient counter-balance swung into action. The mighty supporting Minotaurs lowered their arms; the square slab of solid granite they were holding smashed down on the tiles, obliterating everything beneath.

Toby and Jen had rolled clear as the mighty weight fell to earth. He looked at Jen, not quite believing they had made it. But she was transfixed by something behind them. The magma was quickly seeping across the room, rolling over the granite slab. They could see

4

that the wall had been supporting a magma tunnel that now spewed its contents into the chamber. But there was worse to come.

The earth began to shake. The pressure of the released magma forced a built-up tidal wave of liquid rock to flow from the deeper recesses of the earth.

'Run!' screamed Jen.

Toby followed as fast as he could with the additional weight of the artefact. The magma spewed from the tunnel and across the chamber in a mighty wave that chased them up the incline.

They sped around a corner, the magma splashing after them seconds later. Toby was lagging behind, exhausted.

'Jen! I can't . . . '

She turned to see the corridor behind Toby was nothing more than a wall of superheated rock. She held up her hand and fired her deadly shockwave.

Toby froze—certain that she was going to kill him. By stopping running he knew he was seconds away from being fried alive.

He instinctively ducked as the shockwave passed over his head and destroyed the ceiling behind him. Just when it looked like certain death, the corridor collapsed in a cloud of dust.

'You alive, shrimp?'

A dust cloud rolled up the corridor, dissipating

through the crossroads Jen stood at. There was no movement, which meant the magma had been stopped. But Toby . . .

Toby staggered from the dust, coughing. He slipped his arm around her shoulder and allowed her to lead him out.

Harsh sunlight nearly blinded Toby as they stumbled from a cave overlooking the village. From the smashed rock around him, it was obvious Jen had forced her own entrance into the labyrinth.

They both sat on the grass to catch their breath.

'Thanks,' said Toby.

Jen shrugged. 'I didn't want to have to fish the Dilator from molten magma.'

'Oh,' was all Toby could find to say.

'Thanks for not leaving me to die.'

Toby was offended. 'What do you think I am?'

She looked quizzically at him. 'I think that you're an enigma, Toby Wilkinson. Now, hand it over.'

Toby laughed and tried to stand. Jen was quicker on her feet. She raised her hand as a warning.

'The way I see it is we're almost even, saving each other. But you snatched the last piece. This one's mine.'

Toby was stuck. He knew he couldn't reach his rifle in time. He had no choice.

# Another Piece

'You promise to let me go if I give it to you?'

Jen shrugged. 'This time. Sure.'

Toby slowly reached into his backpack and pulled out a black tube.

'Is that it?' asked Jen suspiciously.

'Duh, no. It's a protective case.'

She took it. Weighed it in her hands. 'I thought you said it was heavy.'

'The case negates the weight. I didn't want to have to drag it around like last time. Twist it open. If you want I'll do it.'

He reached for the tube but she pulled it out of his grasp. 'I can do it myself. Don't you move.'

Toby backed away, hands raised. Jen twisted the top of the tube. It clicked but didn't open. She frowned—then noticed that Toby was smiling and waving at her.

'What have you—?'

There was a loud bang as the teleport-grenade charged up and took Jen on a one-way trip halfway around the world.

Toby cackled over his little trick; it wasn't such a dumb invention after all. He'd forgotten it was in his pack until they were racing through the corridors and he was racking his brain over how he could give Jen the slip.

*Serves her right*, he thought. He walked to the village and made a video-call to Kirby, informing him that the mission was a success. The old man appeared on the screen, looking preoccupied. He nodded, confirmed CUCI lock, and abruptly informed Toby a rescue craft was on its way.

Toby hung up the videoconference. When he looked up his smile vanished.

Pete was sitting on a wall waiting for him.

# Face Off

'Now that's a coincidence,' said Pete, shaking his head.
'I wasn't told it was going to be *you*.'

'What are you doing here, Pete? Are you OK? You
look awful.'

Pete self-consciously stroked his parched cyan cheek.
'I'm better than ever. Look, no glasses, I don't need
them any more.'

'Does that mean you've calmed down now?'

'No. Not at all.'

Pete stood up and advanced towards Toby. Ordinarily
Toby wouldn't have flinched, but there was something
about Pete's poise that seemed aggressive and out of
character. Pete circled him.

'There's a lot of things I don't understand,' said Pete.
'I remember fighting Basilisk at the Hero Foundation,
and then blacking out. What happened after that?'

'You beat him. You did great, mate, a real hero. But
you were covered in raw superpowers and fell into a
coma for about a month.'

'I had bad dreams . . . and good dreams. But I

remember voices . . . distant voices.'

'That was me and the others visiting you.'

'Did my parents come?'

'No, mate. I don't think they know. The Foundation was keeping it all hush-hush.'

Pete looked away, closing his eyes to stop the tears. He regained his composure. 'Where's Emily?'

'I wish I knew. She's been captured . . .' Toby trailed off, he didn't want to tell Pete too much until he was convinced he had regained his senses.

Pete was thoughtful. He gently tapped his head. 'I heard voices. They told me you killed her.'

'Why would I do that? You know me! There's no way I could do that. Listen to yourself. You're hearing voices in your head. Does that sound reasonable? Come back with me and we'll get some help.'

He put his hand on Pete's shoulder in a gesture of solidarity. Pete shrugged him off and glared at him.

'Don't touch me. I have my own life now. I have my own powers. For the first time in my life I have money and freedom to do what I want!' Toby backed off in surprise. There was an unfamiliar confidence in Pete's voice. 'And I've got a job and some surprising new friends. People who respect me and listen to my opinions.' Pete was getting angrier. 'Not like you. You were always trying to take control. You never listened to me!'

'You really have lost it, mate.' Toby shoved past Pete and headed down the slope, towards the village. 'I haven't got time to talk to you. I'm on a *serious* mission. If you come to your senses, give me a call.'

'Wait!'

Toby stopped and turned round; he was angry with Pete. If he could so readily throw aside their friendship then what was the point in talking. Pete held out his hand, and for a moment Toby thought he wanted to shake.

'You have something I need.'

'I don't have anything for you.'

'You have the artefact in your bag. I want it.'

Toby's blood ran cold. He tried to recall what Pete had said about a job. Was he working for the Council of Evil? 'I don't know what you're talking about.'

'Open your bag.' Pete took a threatening step forward. 'Right now I don't feel like kicking your backside all over this island, but I will if you don't hand it over.'

Toby had had enough of the threats. He squared off, nose-to-nose. 'Go to hell, Pete. I need this to save Emily. It's mine.'

'Emily? What's Emily got to do with it?'

'You really are stupid sometimes, Lord—'

Pete's temper snapped. 'Don't call me stupid!'

He slammed both hands into Toby's chest. Toby heard his ribs crunch and he was thrown backwards.

Due to the steep incline the village was built on, Toby sailed clear over one row of houses, but smashed onto the gently curved whitewashed roof of a house in a row further downhill.

A family were having a barbecue under a parasol below him. The sounds of a CD playing bouzouki music masked the noise of his landing. He groaned, feeling his ribs crack back into place thanks to his trusty regeneration power. He heard a thump as Pete landed next to him. He rolled onto his back, partly to see Pete, and partly to stop him from snatching the backpack.

'That hurt!' shouted Toby. He was well aware that once again he had no attack powers, and had to rely on his own wits. He grabbed Pete by the scruff of his neck, planted a foot in his chest and threw him off the roof.

Pete might be superpowered, but the attack was unexpected. He crashed onto the parasol, wrecking the table beneath that was laid with food and drink. He rolled off the table and onto the barbecue. The griddle hissed as his back burnt; he felt his jacket melt. He howled in pain and rolled onto the ground.

A man leaned over Pete, shouting at him in Greek. Pete looked beyond him and saw Toby make a short flight from the rooftop to another.

Pete snarled, pushed the man aside and took to the air—leaving the family to shriek in alarm.

# Face Off

Toby landed on a roof further down the incline. The additional weight from the artefact was turning his flight into a series of long bounds. He glanced round and saw that Pete was flying straight for him. He bounced again to another roof a dozen metres away. This one had a wall that extended, with the cliff dropping to one side. Toby ran along the wall and aimed his rifle. As soon as he touched the grip the device whined to life.

He turned to shoot at Pete—and at that moment the wall crumpled underfoot. Pete had fired an energy blast that dogged Toby's heels. An entire chunk of wall crashed onto a house further down the incline.

Toby managed to turn the fall into a short flight—but he landed awkwardly in the narrow street. With the town sharply rising up the hill he didn't have a clear view of Pete. He wasn't able to out-fly his friend, so he would have to keep low and use the rabbit warren of narrow streets to his advantage.

He sprinted along at street level until he came to a crossroads where the road led sharply up the hill to one side, and steeply down to the cliff edge on the other. He ducked as the wall behind him received the full blast from Pete. The domed-roofed building collapsed in a cloud of dust that obscured Toby. He fired the rifle blindly at Pete.

Pete was forced to zigzag as laser pulses shot from the cloud of debris. When it cleared, Toby had vanished!

Toby sprinted down the street at full pelt. He had taken several side roads, but now headed back towards the sea. Reaching another junction he glanced round— he could see Pete slowly flying over the village, scanning the streets—but he was looking in the opposite direction.

Toby darted across the road, intending to take cover against a wall. Unfortunately he didn't see the pair of Vespa scooters hurtling down the street. Their tinny horns blared and the two drivers swore so rapidly that Toby's Parser couldn't decipher it. One rider managed to skid his scooter sideways—the other slammed into Toby. The rider flipped over the handlebars and clattered on the veranda of a deserted café. The scooter hit Toby at full pelt and both he and the machine rolled down the hill, crashing into a low wall.

The noise was enough to get Pete's attention. He flew overhead. The sight of the flying boy was enough to stop the angry rider from chasing after Toby to retrieve his bike.

Toby wiped blood from his mouth, which healed as he did so. He saw Pete approaching and glanced over the wall he had collided with—it was a straight drop to the sea! He had presumed that there was a harbour. He ducked as a shot from Pete tore a hole through the wall. Toby knew if he fell now, the heavy Dilator piece would take him to the bottom of the sea, and he couldn't out-fly Pete . . .

The hardy scooter engine was still putt-putting. Toby jumped aboard and revved the throttle. The little scooter shot away as the road exploded behind it.

Toby zigzagged across the road to avoid further blasts from Pete. He shot across the ridge. The wall vanished and the side of the road gave way to a sheer drop.

Without looking he fired the gun at the sky behind him, squeezing the trigger until the power-cartridge ran dry. With one hand on the handlebars he couldn't switch the selector to choose another cylinder— another naff design flaw.

He turned a hairpin bend, the rear wheel narrowly avoiding the edge of the ridge. Glancing down, two things struck Toby at once—a small fishing village nestled at the foot of the cliff almost directly below; and, half a mile offshore, there was a magnificent white cruise liner.

Pete swung wide around the hairpin. Toby wasn't moving terribly fast, but he was a small meandering target, and Pete had to admit that he wasn't much of a marksman. Plus he had deliberately been aiming to miss; no matter how much he hated Toby, he didn't want to kill him . . . did he? And he was certain that Toby had been about to tell him something important before he had lost his temper. It was time to change tactics.

A boulder hanging over the road ahead of Toby toppled as Pete shot the dry earth underneath it. The huge rock fell into Toby's path. Toby slammed on the brakes and skidded sideways over the cliff. He rode the Vespa as it arced towards houses in the village below.

Exerting every muscle in his body, he managed to use his power of flight to glide the bike aside—veering away from the houses, and towards the harbour.

He released the handlebars at the very last moment and made the short flight to the ground. He rolled on impact, bouncing across the quay. The scooter slammed into a wooden fishing boat. The entire wooden caique folded in on itself and quickly sank beneath the waves.

Fishermen ran out to investigate the noise—but rapidly backed off as Pete landed on the quay. Toby was on all-fours, crawling away.

Pete was feeling cocky. 'Face it, mate, I'm stronger and faster than you.'

He didn't see that Toby was adjusting the dial on his rifle. Toby rolled onto his back and fired. A blast of amber encased Pete. For once it was a useful assault. Pete couldn't absorb the energy so he didn't grow, and the casing kept him alive but firmly in place. At the very least it bought Toby enough time to escape.

Toby had to get out of the village and await pick up. There was only one road from the village and that was a steep climb back up the cliff. His other option lay on the water. If he could make it to the cruise ship, he stood a better chance of hiding. He scanned the harbour for anything he could use . . .

Pete tensed every muscle and invoked another superpower. After a few seconds he heard the satisfying sound of his prison cracking.

The cowering fishermen watched in astonishment as the amber shattered as flames erupted from Pete's body. He stood in the centre of the village and bellowed victoriously. The flames extinguished with a dull whump, leaving no obvious signs of damage to him.

'Toby?' Pete yelled as he looked around. There were dozens of places he could be concealed. 'There's no use hiding. Look, just give me the thing and I'll leave you alone. I've got better things to do! Places to rob, possessions to buy!'

He pushed over a stack of empty crates; then yanked away a tarpaulin from a boat. No Toby. He looked up when he heard the faint sounds of a motor.

Toby was skimming across the bay on a jet ski; he was already halfway to the cruise liner. Pete couldn't help but feel a trace of envy: despite all the amazing things he could do, *that* looked fun.

Toby clung on for life as the jet ski bounced clear out of the water each time it traversed a wave. He was trying to intercept the cruise liner, but it was moving

much faster than him. An almighty splash to port sig-
nalled that Pete was shooting at him again.

Toby coaxed the jet ski as close as he could to the
cruise liner. Up close, the vessel was huge, a wall of
white metal that curved gracefully from the sea. It was
a wonder that something so heavy could float.

The powerful bow waves that rolled from the side of
the liner caused Toby to buck high out of the water
making him a more difficult target for Pete. But no
matter how hard Toby throttled the jet ski, the cruiser
was slipping away from him. He steeled himself, then
shot into the air as fast as he could.

Toby knew it was a matter of seconds before the
heavy artefact would weigh him down, but he needed
to make it onto the deck. It was a close call—after thirteen decks, he reached the top, slowing to a halt as
gravity clawed at him—but luck was with him as he
felt the upper deck beneath his trainers.

He was amidships; a large swimming pool took up
the deck, packed with lazing holidaymakers. Waiters
drifted between them serving drinks. Nobody had
noticed Toby's unorthodox arrival. Through the crowds
of people, he saw Pete appear towards the stern. He
had chosen a surreptitious arrival rather than cause a
panic aboard, although his appearance caused a few
heads to turn. Pete saw Toby and started pushing his
way through the crowd.

Toby bolted for a doorway and ran down a plush corridor. Tourists in front of him quickly parted, with alarmed expressions. A door slammed behind him, which meant Pete was catching up.

The layout of the liner was no less complicated than the labyrinth he had just escaped from. A staircase spiralled from this deck, linking several decks below, casinos and shops branched off at every level—it was like being inside a shopping centre. Toby leapt from the balcony, using his flight powers to soften his landing.

Pete followed, but Toby was a fraction faster. More guests parted as he sprinted down the corridors. He caught glimpses of terrified faces as he passed.

He pushed through a door and found himself in a spacious kitchen, busy with over a dozen chefs preparing meals. A grouchy looking chef waved his ladle at Toby.

'You, boy! Get outta here!'

Pete kicked the door open and scanned the kitchen. Everybody froze. What disease was this blue-tinged boy bringing into the hygienic kitchen? Pete fired and Toby leapt for cover as a rack of pans above his head were hit.

Chefs scattered for cover as chaos broke out. Toby tried to shoot back but his rifle had drained the amber charge. He flicked the selector and squeezed the trigger.

Lightning forked across the countertops—flinging Pete across a worktop, scattering ingredients. Toby climbed to his feet and crossed to Pete; he was concerned that the blast might have been too much.

'Pete?'

Pete stood up—towering thirty centimetres over a stunned Toby.

'Bad idea!' snarled Pete flexing his expanded muscles.

Pete raised his hands to shoot. Toby acted on instinct—he grabbed a large pan of boiling water and flung it over his former friend. Pete screamed in pain as his skin hissed and turned red. Toby bolted. A stove next to him was blown apart as he made it through the swing doors—

Straight into a busy dining room. All heads turned his way—and then they screamed in unison. Toby realized why everybody had given him a wide berth as he'd run down the corridors. He'd been waving his gun.

'Pirates!' somebody yelled in panic.

'No! It's—'

The door behind him flew off its hinges. Toby didn't need to look. He ran through the rows of tables. Pete lumbered after him firing blast after blast. Tables and diners were flung everywhere and screams filled the air.

Toby tried to shake Pete off by turning down every side-passage he came to. He ran through a door and found himself on a fire escape. The stairs led up as well as down. He had planned to ascend—but then felt an energy bolt hit his shoulder. He rolled down the stairwell head-first. Without his powers to save him, he would have broken his neck.

Toby got to his feet and continued down. It was an almost comical chase—the staircase provided so much cover that it meant that neither boy could use their powers.

Toby reached the bottom, convinced he must be below the waterline. The corridor had changed from wide luxury to narrow utilitarian. Pipes ran along the ceiling, and fluorescent lights flickered. He ran but there was nowhere to hide. Another blast from Pete knocked the wind out of him and he fell against the hull. Toby gasped for breath and felt his stomach churn; he thought he must be hurt pretty badly. He was also aware that water was trickling in from the hull under his cheek.

Pete loomed over him and grabbed the backpack. 'You could have just given me the damn thing. But you had to think you were better than me.' Toby was too winded to reply. 'You were going to tell me something back on the island. Something about Emily?'

Toby felt a loathing for Pete, something he had never felt before. Doc Tempest had kidnapped his mother, and Basilisk had taken Pete—all things that had made Toby angry. But this was different. This was not some random villain threatening him. This was his friend. It was *personal*. He found his voice.

'I was going to tell you . . . that she *hates* your guts and she hoped you'd died in that coma.' He regretted the words as soon as he'd spoken them.

Pete stared at Toby, his voice trembling with hostility. 'I'm going to leave here now. You're not going to follow me, or I might change my mind about not wanting to kill you.' He turned and started walking away.

Toby shook his head. 'You're not leaving here with the artefact.'

Pete stopped. The lack of emotion on his face was somehow alarming.

'You always wanted to play the hero, didn't you? Well, now you can choose. The artefact, or save the people on this sinking ship.' He placed both fists together and fired a dual blast at the damaged hull behind Toby. Metal groaned as the double hull was punctured and seawater began flooding the cruise liner!

In seconds an alarm had sounded, the captain barking orders to 'Abandon ship'.

The blast of the water knocked Toby off his feet and swept him down the corridor. When he managed to stand he saw the corridor was rapidly filling up—and Pete was nowhere to be seen.

# Consequences

Pete held the artefact he had snatched from Toby up to the light, examining it from every angle. He couldn't guess what it actually was. He paced his hotel room and glanced at the clock. Then everything seemed to wobble and the revolving second hand froze. Pete could sense a presence, but couldn't see anybody.

'You're late,' he said as he looked around the room.

'I arrive when I intend to therefore I am *always* on time.'

'Well, your on time is five minutes later than you said.'

'You have the item?'

The air seemed to fog slightly and a tall thin man stepped from nowhere: Lord Eon. He was almost seven feet tall, pale skinned with neat dark hair and a neat beard. He looked about thirty, except for some deep creases on his face that belonged to an old man. He was dressed in an immaculate black suit.

Pete held the Temporal Dilator up. 'There you go.'

Eon's eyes went wide, but he made no motion to take it. 'You have performed superbly. You truly deserve your rich reward.'

Pete smiled. Praise and a reward, that's what the Foundation should have been heaping on him.

Eon made a sweeping gesture with his hand and the fabric of space was ripped apart as a small vortex appeared in the room. Pete watched with interest as individual atoms from the furniture were drawn towards it, bending completely out of shape like a surreal painting.

'Cool black hole,' said Pete. 'Can I get that power?'

'Close. It's a gravastar. Throw the artefact inside.'

Pete was surprised. 'You want to destroy it?'

'I merely want you to place it in the gravastar. Careful! Don't get too close.'

Pete tossed the artefact inside. It seemed to stretch incredibly thin as it fell. Eon closed the vortex with a clap of his hands.

'Why did you do that? Come to mention it, what was it?'

Eon closed his hands and the object vanished. 'You ask too many questions, Mr Kendall. Why make life complicated? I have what I want, and you will have what you want. I have secured an island property for you off the coast of Cuba. It's all yours.'

Pete's eyes lit up. 'Really?'

# Consequences

'Of course. I will have use for you again, but until then . . . enjoy the fruits of your work.'

Pete took a step forward—the hotel carpet instantly became white sand and the walls melted away to blinding sunlight. There was none of the sense of travel that he got with teleportation. He simply *was* somewhere else.

He shaded his eyes and looked across the sandy bay. An emerald green lagoon lay beyond. Behind was a huge perfectly preserved colonial mansion. And it was all his.

Pete laughed out loud and gave a little victory dance on the beach—*his* beach. All his life he had strived to do the right thing, especially when he and his friends had discovered Hero.com, and where had it got him? Now, after the briefest of crimewaves he had his own tropical island. Whoever said crime didn't pay had never tried it.

Pete walked into his mansion. His footsteps echoed on the pine floorboards. It was peaceful and quiet. He was completely alone.

A crushing weight lay on Toby's chest. Now that the battle with Pete was over, the anger he'd felt against his old friend had disappeared. It was replaced first by a heavy sadness. Losing Pete's friendship was like losing a brother. The sense of sadness was chased away by guilt. If Toby hadn't been so stubborn and such a control freak, Pete wouldn't have felt that Hero.com was being taken away from him and they would still be friends, fighting side-by-side to save Emily . . . her name conjured another bout of remorse. To save the world, he corrected himself.

Toby's emotions raged. He sat in Kirby's office alone, staring at the map. When he had insisted on returning home to see his parents and have a rest, Kirby had flatly refused. Toby had lost his temper and demanded to see Lorna. Again his request was denied.

Something was going on that he wasn't privy to, and he didn't like it. So far this mission had almost killed him several times, and he had yet to face Lord Eon, the enemy he was supposed to be fighting. Instead he had just fought his best friend. He remembered Lorna's words—would he sacrifice his friends to do the right thing? After battling Pete he had the nagging suspicion that he would. What kind of friend did that make him?

Toby had frantically tried to save the cruise liner as it lurched in the sea. Everybody was on deck, running for lifeboats. It was chaos and still no sign of the Foundation transport to help. He had used his phone to try to download more powers to save the sinking liner, but had been alarmed to see a banner flashing across the screen saying: ACCESS DENIED.

# Consequences

He made a vid-call to Kirby and explained the situation. The old man went bonkers when Toby said he had lost the Dilator segment, and before he could explain any further he was teleported straight back to Kirby's office.

Toby had frantically insisted they should return and help save the liner, but Kirby silenced him and gave assurances that the Foundation had heroes on the job. He was far more concerned with how Toby had lost the artefact. He listened intently then shook his head sadly.

'So the Council of Evil have a piece, and we have two,' said Toby. 'Is that so much of a problem? You said it was the Council that helped imprison Eon last time. We could work with them for the common good.'

'Indeed. But your pal isn't working for the Council. He's working for Lord Eon himself.'

'How can you know that?'

'We have . . . spies in all the right places. I assure you, Kendall has made a pig's ear of things. We have a piece, the enemy has a piece, and now Eon has a piece.'

Toby frowned. 'The Council has a piece? And I thought we had two? What about the one in the armoured car?'

Kirby looked blankly at him for a second. 'Yes, that one. It was stolen from our holding cell. It seems not everybody around here is to be trusted. I thought you would have realized that after fighting your friend.' The snippy comment hurt Toby.

Kirby had then left to see if the mess could be salvaged. He made no effort to disguise the fact he blamed Toby for everything going wrong.

That had been almost two hours ago. Toby had tried to sleep on a sofa, but couldn't. His mind was too active. What wasn't he being told? He felt as though his missions were more than they seemed, but how?

Feeling hungry, he tried to open the door, but the keypad wouldn't respond. It probably only worked for Kirby since this was his private office. Toby walked around the desk; it was too new to be cluttered, and there were no snacks hidden in the empty drawers.

He thumbed the remote control on the plasma screen hoping to get a TV channel, but it wouldn't budge from the world map. He noticed a small crack in the corner of the screen and wondered if Kirby had thumped the screen in one of the fits of anxiety he seemed to be having lately.

With a sigh, and desperate to distract his inner-thoughts from their depressing monologues, he sat down in Kirby's chair and tried to log on to the computer. It was switched off. Thumbing the power button got him nowhere. He checked the power cable was plugged into the monitor; it was there all right. But the other end wasn't plugged in. In fact there was no power socket at all. A quick check at the back of the computer revealed that nothing was plugged in.

'Great,' he muttered. He was starting to get a panicky feeling, as though he was being kept in the room on purpose. That made him determined to get out, even though he had no powers and his equipment had been taken back into storage.

He got up and re-examined the keypad on the wall by the door. It was a touch screen that not only reacted to the correct code, but also scanned the fingerprint of the person as they typed to ensure they were known. Next he turned his attention to the door itself.

A quick rap with his knuckles revealed it to be thick metal. If only he had enhanced strength, he could prise it open. He dug his fingernails in the narrow gap and pulled; although he knew it would be a futile gesture . . .

The door rolled effortlessly open. Toby gaped. It was indeed thick metal, but it opened by rolling along a groove in the floor and had no actual locking mechanism. Kirby had told him that the place was new, but this was ridiculous.

The door opened into an empty corridor. Toby crept out. He didn't know why he was being so cautious; after all, he worked here. However, he had no intention of provoking the old man's temper, which had been at breaking point since this whole Eon crisis had begun.

He walked to a large blast door that sealed one end of the corridor. This one proved immobile. His stomach was rumbling; there had to be a canteen around here somewhere. Defeated, he backtracked and turned a corner. It was a T-junction. Ahead there was another door sealing him in; a bored looking guard slouched in a chair playing on a PSP, earphones in. Metres before the guard was a short side passage that ended in a door that Toby did recognize: the equipment room.

The guard didn't look up as Toby quietly sneaked towards him and slipped into the side passage. He paused outside the equipment room. He could hear voices from inside.

'This operation is getting out of hand!' said an unfamiliar voice.

'Once again I'm telling you that Toby is the best suited for this job! There is nobody else we can trust after everything that has gone on here; we need him.' That was Eric Kirby's voice. Toby smiled, glad that Kirby still held him in high regard.

He peeked into the room but could only see Kirby pacing inside.

'After what happened in Greece—'

'The other agents were a known commodity, something that the boy handled skilfully. The situation with the Kendall boy was completely unexpected.'

# Consequences

Even though Toby was bitter about what Pete had done, he still took offence that they were referring to him as 'the Kendall' boy. After all, Pete had been equally vital in preserving the Hero Foundation as he had been.

'There is one piece remaining. That we *must* have.'

'But we still don't know where to look,' complained Kirby.

'I'm authorizing all satellite resources be focused on the job.'

There had been something troubling Toby about the conversation, and now he knew what it was. The unseen person was giving Kirby orders. As far as he was aware, Kirby had created and owned the Foundation. This conversation meant there were people *above* him. More powerful ones . . .

Kirby's voice focused his attention. 'That's what I've been asking for all along. And once we retrieve the last segment?'

'We'll figure out how to proceed. If worst comes to worst we will have to liaise with the enemy.'

'And Kendall?'

'He needs to be eliminated.'

Toby's blood ran cold. His emotions were already on a rollercoaster, but he didn't want to hear *that*.

'Perhaps Toby could do the honours? He knows how Kendall thinks, and what to expect.'

They wanted him to kill his best friend? Toby's mind was racing.

'He has powerful allies,' warned Kirby.

'Then we will have to bring them down too.'

Toby heard Kirby shuffling for the door, his cane tapping on the floor. He didn't want to be caught eavesdropping. He tiptoed past the guard and around the corner as he heard the door slide open. Kirby's footsteps quickly echoed down the corridor.

Toby ducked back into the office and slid the door closed. He was sweating by now. He quickly scanned the office to make sure it didn't seem as though he had been snooping, then jumped back onto the sofa as the door rolled open.

Kirby looked at him with a frown. 'Are you OK? Your face is red.'

Toby faked a smile. 'I'm fine. It's just a bit hot in here and I'm starving.'

'I'll get some food brought in. Unfortunately the air conditioning is not working, but I'll get some cold drinks too. We are intensifying our search for the last piece of the Temporal Dilator. As soon as we pick up a temporal dilation, it's imperative that you are ready for deployment.'

Toby was bursting to know who Kirby's boss was, but knew he couldn't say anything. 'It would be better if I downloaded attack powers directly, rather than rely on

# Consequences

these gadgets. It's simply not practical. Those proto-types have nearly got me killed several times already!'

Kirby shook his head. 'As I have said before, we must control your downloading of attack powers. This is the best way.'

'But if this mission is so critical—'

'ENOUGH!' snapped Kirby. The brief flash of anger across Kirby's face startled Toby. 'They are the rules. Full stop.'

*He must be under a lot of pressure*, thought Toby. He lowered his gaze. He understood that Kirby would be as stressed as he was over the instructions to kill Pete, and acting like a prima donna wasn't going to help.

'Eon has struck again.'

'Where?'

'Zurich, Switzerland. He's gone quickly from small towns to a major city.' Kirby zoomed in on a red spot that was pulsing on the map. Toby hadn't noticed it earlier as he'd been more interested in trying to find a TV channel. He felt stupid; he should have been alert.

'How many people?'

'Approximately three hundred and eight thousand people. His biggest attack yet.'

Toby felt a shudder of panic. 'Dead?'

'As good as. Eon is like a vulture scavenging their time. Like Emily, they are gone, trapped between the ticks of the clock.'

# HERO.CØM

'Why Zurich?'

Kirby shrugged. 'Because they make excellent clocks there? Who knows? His attacks are randomly spread across the globe. We know Eon is not motivated by money. He desires to grow more powerful by feeding from mankind's chronons. We must stop him before it gets worse.'

Kirby turned back to the screen. 'If he knew where we were the consequences would be disastrous. Even we, with all our powers, would be defenceless against the master of time.'

*Yet all we can do is wait*, thought Toby. *How ironic.*


In any other circumstances, gentle waves lapping on snow-white sand on your own tropical paradise island would be perfection.

However, Pete was deeply bored.

He had walked around his island. Or, rather more accurately, he had stepped through the front door of his mansion and out of the back door to find himself on the opposite side of the island. It wasn't so much an island as an atoll with a few palm trees. Inside, the television was one of the biggest he had ever seen, but it lacked the basic aerial or satellite dish, so showed nothing but a signal-less blue screen. Even the fridge was empty. Lord Eon had been less than thorough in

44

fulfilling his end of the bargain; although he couldn't imagine the supervillain strolling down the aisle of a supermarket pushing a trolley with a wonky wheel as he stocked up with food.

Worse than all that, though, was that Pete had nobody to talk to. He couldn't pick up the phone and invite Toby, Lorna, and Emily around because a) he didn't have a phone and b) he didn't have any friends.

Where had his life gone so wrong? *At birth*, he thought darkly. He shook those thoughts away. They were a path to depression. He had to admit that fighting Toby had been enjoyable. It was like play fighting on a grand scale. Pete didn't feel the slightest remorse for sinking the cruise ship. He knew that what he had done was an act of supreme evil. Basilisk would be proud of him. The old Pete would have been wallowing in guilt. But for the new Pete, it was as though he could now observe his emotions from a distance. He could impassively watch as he performed unspeakable acts, and the only thing he would feel was a curiosity as to *why* he felt so numb. Being soaked in the morass of superpowers must have melted his moral compass. On an intellectual level he knew his actions were wrong, but inside . . . he simply didn't care.

Toby could be dead. He let that thought circulate in his mind. Nothing, not the slightest twinge of emotion. Perhaps he should see a psychiatrist? He knew that was the first thing Emily would have said to him. He liked the way she spoke her mind. The thought of Emily brought with it a complex rush of emotions. So he *could* still feel something. That was a start.

Jake stepped from the shadows. There had been no teleportation bang. Pete wondered how long he had been there, watching him go slowly mad.

'Hunter! How did you find me?'

Jake pulled something from behind his back. Pete leapt from the overstuffed couch he had been lying on, hand raised to fire—

Jake held up a pizza box. 'Whoa! Easy now. If that's how you treat the delivery guy, I don't think you'll be leaving a tip.'

He put the box on the table and Pete eagerly started to pull the cheesy slices apart. He had taken a mouthful before he realized that Jake wasn't eating.

Jake laughed at the expression on Pete's face. 'Do you really think I'm trying to poison you? I've already eaten.' Jake sat opposite him and watched as Pete's mouth mechanically chewed, suspicion never leaving Pete's face. 'I told you, I want to be friends now.'

'After everything you've done to me?'

Jake shrugged. 'We were kids then.'

'It was only a couple of months ago!'

'Yeah, but look at us now, eating pizza in paradise! And this is all yours, I believe.'

# Consequences

'Who told you?'

'I have my contacts at the Council. In fact, I've got quite a good position there. I've been shaking things up. It will soon be time for a new change in management, so to speak. When that happens I think you'll find there's a place for you there. Somewhere you're in control and not the stupid Hero Foundation.'

Pete was curious, but contented himself with another mouthful of pizza. He noticed Jake was pulling a face.

'Whu—?' he said with a full mouth.

Jake unconsciously rubbed his own cheek. 'What's wrong with your skin? You're falling into your pizza.'

Pete looked at his hands. Large flakes of skin, the size of coins, dropped onto the pizza. He threw the slice down. More skin fell off. It didn't hurt, but it was pretty disgusting. He could see blisters rapidly forming to replace the chunks.

'I'm falling apart.'

'I'm sure you'll regenerate,' said Jake, staring at the now disgusting-looking pizza.

Pete's skin problem had become worse over the last day, and didn't appear to be healing.

Jake got back to business. 'Listen, how would you like to come with me to the Council HQ? It's an island . . . little bigger than this.'

The idea sounded appealing. Pete knew that the precise location of the Council of Evil's base was a closely

guarded secret. The Foundation was constantly searching for it. Plus, Pete still didn't know whether his powers were permanent. If they were to fade away, he
would need to download more from somewhere. He
tried to hide his enthusiasm.

'Why would I want to do that?'

'I need somebody like you around. Somebody I can
trust. There are people who would like to see me gone.'

Now Pete laughed. 'What makes you think you can
trust me?'

'Can't I? I thought I was the untrustworthy one. Or
did I get that wrong? Like I said, I need somebody like
you. I can't do what I'm planning on my own.' Jake
hated saying that, but it was true. In part.

Pete couldn't believe that somebody actually needed
him. After tagging along with Toby, who took him for
granted, being needed was something he longed to
hear—and Jake Hunter was the last person he had
expected to hear it from. He tried to act calmly, but his
face showed the excitement he felt.

'OK. What have I got to lose?'

Jake smiled. 'Thanks. And since you have chosen to
trust me, there's something you need to know. Lord
Eon is using you.'

Pete blinked in surprise. How did Jake know he had
been working with Eon?

'I know he asked you to retrieve an artefact for him.

# Consequences

That artefact is part of an ancient weapon that can be used against him.'

Was this a trick? Pete didn't know what to believe.

'I also know he's going to use you to get the last piece. If you deliver the last piece to him . . . well, let's just say the world will face a major crisis—and it won't matter whose side you are on. Nobody will be able to stop him. In fact, it could be the one moment that the good guys and bad guys . . . and everybody in between, will have to work together or face certain annihilation.'

Pete stared hard at him. Then laughed. 'Is this a joke?'

Jake solemnly shook his head. 'The consequences of doing nothing are . . . ' Jake couldn't think of a word to describe the absolutely pressing urgency of the problem. ' . . . bad,' he finished lamely. 'Already ambassadors from both sides have started to talk. They're calling it the Crisis Point—the end of civilization as we know it. Everybody trapped in time and space and only Lord Eon left running the show.'

'I don't believe you. This is a trick. You want me to get the last piece and give it to you.'

'It's not a trick. But you're right, I want that piece.'

'Do I look stupid?'

Jake fought every fibre of his being *not* to remain silent. 'Of course not,' he said in the sincerest voice he could muster. 'I used to call you professor because you were clever. Much smarter than me.' Jake was relieved that his self-effacing comment seem to calm Pete.

'True. So, in helping him . . . I've just helped in destroying the world?'

'Yep. Pretty wild, huh? Lord Eon is a manipulator. He not only manipulates time and space, but people. He rewarded you with this island because it means nothing to him. Stopping anybody else from getting their hands on the final bit of the only machine that can stop him is worth more to him than all the money in the world.'

Pete was still unsure what to make of what he was hearing. He could see Jake was serious, but how much of that was merely an act? And how could he suddenly start trusting someone who had made his life so miserable? Then again, hadn't Toby been about to mention something too?

'He destroyed the piece of the Temporal Dilator I gave him,' said Pete.

Jake nodded thoughtfully. 'Maybe one piece can be replicated. But if he gets his hands on another . . . ' Jake stood up and paced the room. Pete noticed that he kept to the shadows. 'What have you been told about that girl you like, what's her name? Emily?'

Pete didn't like Jake poking around his personal life. 'She's a friend.'

'Sure she is. But what do you know?'

# Consequences

Pete hesitated. 'I was told . . . I thought I was told that Toby killed her.' He recalled the voices he'd heard deep in his coma. That was the spark that had finally lit his rage. He also remembered Lorna's voice. She had confirmed that Emily was dead.

No. That was wrong. He thought harder. Tried to recall Lorna's voice in the darkness. She had said that Emily was *missing*. Not dead. And Toby had looked confused too when Pete challenged him in hospital.

'Lord Eon took her,' said Jake.

That piece of news was like a slap across the face. 'What?'

Jake sighed heavily. 'Forget what you may have been told before. What I'm telling you now is the truth.'

'But . . . but . . . why would he do that? Why Emily?'

'He has been taking individuals from all over the place and now that he's growing in power, his targets are getting bigger. He took Emily because she was unconscious when he arrived to try and intercept one of the pieces of this machine. She was a victim like everybody else. But in this case I think she was taken for another reason too. This all sounds weird, but I've been told that what we do *now* can affect events in the past. Wild, huh?'

Pete didn't bat an eyelid. He read a lot of science fiction, but he also loved reading about new breakthroughs in science. Although he didn't really understand half the stuff he read, he recalled an experiment called 'the double split' that had proved that action now can affect events in the past.

Jake pressed on. 'Anyway, it could be that she was taken to provoke you into doing something . . . in the past.'

Now Pete was confused.

Jake grinned and held up his hands. 'I'm only telling you what I've been told. I didn't really get it all. But importantly, she is alive. And she can only be released if Eon is stopped.' Jake could see that Pete was shocked. It was a lot of information to process—but they didn't have the luxury of time. 'Come on, we need to go on a little trip.'

'Are we going to the Council now?'

Jake smiled and waved his hand. A shimmering portal opened up in the air, a quantum tunnel to their destination.

'Not yet. You need to see what your boss is capable of. We're going to Switzerland.'

# Beat the Bullet

Toby had been on tenterhooks waiting for the satellites to pick up any chronological anomaly. When they finally did, Kirby suspected that there was a lag on the signal they were receiving—a deliberate sabotage attempt by the enemy. This seemed to tip him into panic and he had rushed his selection of Toby's down-loadable powers. Now, Toby had no clear idea what he had been given. At one point in the process he heard Kirby uncharacteristically swear and had felt a sharp tingle in his body, as though he had been given more than three powers.

Then Toby had been ushered into the equipment room, been handed a bag of gadgets, and had a small pistol holstered to his belt. Next he had been shoved onto the teleport pad, with no time to ask a single question.

Toby had arrived in a bare concrete basement, lit by a single light bulb. There was no clue as to where he was. After the jungle ruins of Cambodia and the sub-terranean labyrinths of ancient Greece, this wasn't exactly the kind of environment he'd been expecting. A single door led from the room. With Kirby's incessant warnings that they might be too late ringing in his ears, Toby walked through it.

He found himself in a huge room. Massive steel columns rose to the ceiling and behind him a steel staircase spiralled up to a hatch in the ceiling. Toby guessed that he was in the foundations of a large building, but what impressed him most was the archaeological treasure that poked from the dirt.

The ground had been carefully excavated, revealing what looked like ancient Japanese ruins. Toby could make out the distinctive uplifted corners of a wooden hipped-gable roof. The top level of the building had been cleared, and electric lights strung inside illuminated the rest of a pagoda, which ran several storeys underground.

*It must be here*, thought Toby as he checked his phone, activating the chrono-scanner. A faint blip appeared. He swept the device left and right and frowned as the signal grew stronger to his right, *away* from the ruins. Then he angled the device upwards—the signal got stronger still.

'Oh no . . . ' muttered Toby under his breath. Somebody had already beaten him to it and, judging by the moving blip, was running away from him.

Toby raced up the staircase and pushed open the

hatch. It led to a cordoned-off area of an underground car park. He hesitated at the sight before him—several vehicles were on fire, some resting on their roofs. Choking black smoke stung his eyes. Dozens of car alarms sang their ear-splitting song. The destruction was not Lord Eon's *modus operandi*—that meant that the Council of Evil had got here first but who had they been fighting if Toby was the first hero on the scene?

Toby covered his mouth with his jacket and ran up the exit ramp. He reached the street, coughing and spluttering. A large crowd had assembled around the building and he could hear the sounds of approaching fire engines. The gathered crowd gave the first indications of where he was, but what took his breath away was the massive metropolis spread out before him.

Huge buildings lined streets that were densely packed with cars and crowds of people who crossed the roads on super-wide pedestrian walkways. Billboards covered in Japanese writing filled every available space. Huge glass and steel skyscrapers dominated the end of the street. A name on one, emblazed in red neon, caught his eye: Tokyo.

Away from the smoke, the smell and noise of the mega-city assaulted his senses; it was overwhelming. Toby tried to focus on the task in hand and examined his scanner. The Temporal Dilator was moving, but it wasn't far away. Toby looked around for a quiet place he could launch into flight, but there was nowhere for him to do it discreetly.

He ran forwards, hoping that he had some kind of super-speed, only to find that he was running on empty. The crowds were massive; he had never seen so many people in one place. He pushed forward and turned a corner—his target lay dead ahead.

A loud boom caught his attention. He looked up to see a blue and white bus spinning through the air—straight for him! It crashed on to several cars and rolled towards him in a shower of twisted metal and broken glass.

Toby raised his hands, hoping that some kind of defensive power would kick in. The bus filled his vision. A jet of ice shot from his palms, creating a curved shield in front of him. The bus slammed to a halt against the ice. Toby gave a satisfied smile—which dropped seconds later as the ice shield shattered from both the weight of the bus and the humidity in the city. The vehicle slammed down on top of him.

Luck was with him. He was standing directly under a shattered window. He opened his eyes to find himself standing in the centre of the sidelong bus. People lay inside at odd angles and he could hear screaming and sobbing. He knew he should help the injured, but another explosion from outside made him realize that he was still in danger. Toby raised his hand skyward, to the broken window opposite, and launched into flight—

Or rather jumped out of the bus and landed outside. With a sense of dread he realized that, in his haste, Kirby hadn't downloaded a flying power, only a jumping ability.

Hordes of people had gathered around the bus, trying to free those inside. His Parser buzzed with concerned offers of help. Toby pinballed through the crowd. Ahead he could see a plume of smoke from the explosion he'd heard—and yet more crowds of people were screaming as they fled the unseen battle. If he wanted to run *into* danger then he was going the right way.

Sliding across the bonnet of a car, Toby saw what was happening. The traffic had cleared around an intersection where Jen was crouching. She had something in her backpack, which she kept a hand on. Her other hand was splayed open, red energy crackling between her fingers. She was bleeding and looked rough as she fired her shockwave. But it wasn't aimed at Toby.

Her opponent was three and a half metres tall and jerked as the blast hit him. Energy surged over rippling muscles that swelled under the black jumpsuit he was wearing, which expanded as he absorbed the energy, growing an extra half metre. It was Pete. Toby knew that each blast Jen was delivering was making his friend more powerful.

'No!' he screamed.

Both Jen and Pete looked round—both firing at him at the same time. Toby raised his hands to conjure protection—it only partially worked. An ice shield formed but was instantly disintegrated by Jen's shockwave, which allowed Pete's pyrokinetic ball to hit him firmly in the chest.

The breath was sucked from his lungs as they collapsed. Toby was carried fifteen metres across the street and through the second storey window of a tower block. He felt his spine being pummelled as he bounced off several office desks, smashing monitors as he went.

He lay in a huddle on the floor, unable to move. For thirty seconds he could only hear the sound of cricking bones as his healing power pressed his body back into shape. He was on the verge of black-out by the time his lungs healed, finally allowing him to take a deep breath. He climbed unsteadily to his feet and looked out of the broken window.

Jen and Pete were continuing their battle further down the street. It was utter destruction. He watched as Pete threw Jen through a plate glass window and into a car showroom. *Serves the villain right*, thought Toby. But his emotions were torn because Pete was his enemy too. He couldn't really champion either of them, and it looked as if he'd have to fight them both.

# Beat the Bullet

'Dammit!' snarled Toby. The powers Kirby had given him seemed next to useless. He used his phone to access Hero.com.

A message flashed up: ACCESS DENIED.

He thumped the device in anger. What was wrong with this piece of junk? He looked around the office and saw that several computers were still in operation in the far corner. His inbuilt CUCI could bypass any security needed to log-on to the machine and he would be taken directly to Hero.com where he could download more powers.

The log-on screen demanding a username and password glitched as the CUCI wirelessly seized control. The browser appeared—but again Hero.com refused him access. This was ridiculous! There was no way he could face two supervillains with only the powers he had now.

He hit the videoconference icon on his phone and called Kirby. A message flashed: SERVICE UNAVAILABLE.

Toby had to stop himself from throwing the phone against the wall. He was completely out of touch with the Foundation, with no back-up, no flying or teleport powers—in fact with no powers of any real use! When he returned he would have to have a serious word with Eric Kirby.

Toby drew his pistol and checked it out. It was like

the rifle but on a smaller scale. A green LED flashed on the butt; tiny lettering indicated it was a Wi-Fi signal. That was something at least: in theory he wouldn't run out of ammunition.

Toby jumped from the window and bounded into the intersection. Another bound brought him right into the middle of the fight. This time he wasn't going to waste time with warnings. He shot at Jen, and took great satisfaction from sending her sprawling to the ground. At the same time he had his other hand raised and formed an ice shield as Pete swung a punch at him.

'Pete! Wait! I don't want to fight you!'

Pete splintered the ice shield with a second punch, and then glared down at Toby. Toby was intimidated. Pete looked fearsome, and, at twice normal size, unbeatable.

'If you don't want to fight, then you've got ten seconds to get out of here,' growled Pete in an unnaturally deep voice.

'Pete, listen to me. I know you're working for Eon. I know you want the artefact Jen has—but Eon can't have it.'

'*Nine!*'

'If he gets it there's no way to stop him. He'll be free to destroy the world as we know it.'

'*Eight!*'

'The Foundation won't be able to stop him. The

# Beat the Bullet

Council of Evil won't be able to stop him—and you will be powerless too!'

'I know all that! *Seven!*'

Toby was confused. 'Then if you know it—'

'*Six!*'

'Why are you doing this if you know it will mean the end of everybody—including you!'

'I've warned you! *Five!*'

'Pete—'

'Where'd she go?'

Toby looked around. Jen was nowhere to be seen. A quick glance at the scanner revealed that she was close by, unable to teleport while she had the artefact. It occurred to him that Pete didn't have a scanner, so all Toby had to do was give him the slip.

'I knew it!' Pete growled. 'You're working with her!'

'With her? Why would I be working with the Council?'

WHAM! Toby didn't even see Pete's fist until it hit his nose. The impact carried him over the traffic. It took him so long to land that his nose had regenerated mid-flight.

Toby landed on a taxi roof with a crunch. Luckily the attack had moved him closer to Jen. Pete tried to launch himself into the air, but his heavy mass dragged him back down to earth. For once Toby had the advantage with his leaping ability. In three bounds he had doubled the distance between himself and Pete.

He followed the scanner as Jen turned down another street, heading eastwards. Unable to fly, she must be trying to get to someone or something that could get her out of the country.

Toby reached a junction where the road curved north and south around what looked like a river or lake; beyond that was a wooded park. He saw that Jen was running southwards. One jump and he could cut her off. Then he heard a familiar angry bellow.

Pete vaulted from an overhead road bridge that joined the main boulevard. Cars honked their horns and swerved around him. He landed in front of Jen, tarmac cracking under his weight. Jen screamed as she scrambled to a halt.

Pete raised his arms to shoot her but was distracted as a van skidded straight into him, its engine exploding in a cloud of smoke.

Toby rationalized the situation. The main villain here was Eon. He wanted the artefact most. If Toby was forced to choose sides now he should help Jen to escape with the final piece of the Dilator. It went against every fibre of Toby's being, but that was the right choice.

He need not have worried. Jen still had her wits about her. She changed direction and ran straight for the river, clumsily climbing over the roadside fence.

# Beat the Bullet

Toby watched as she cupped her hand around a Bluetooth headset she was wearing. He heard her shout, 'Light Bridge!'

The headset glowed as it downloaded a superpower. Toby was impressed.

Jen extended both arms as she ran. A silver light threaded its way across the water, forming a bridge of light.

Pete tried to follow, but the crumpled car wrapped around his leg hampered his movements.

Toby ran for the river—he was unsure if he could leap *that* far. He launched himself centimetres from the water's edge. He reached the wooded island at the same time Jen did.

She shrieked as Toby landed next to her. Then her eyes narrowed.

'You—' The profanity was lost as she fired her shock-wave. Toby hit the deck just in time.

'Stop! I've got a proposition for you!'

Jen stood over him, hands blazing with energy. 'What could I possibly want from you?'

'A truce. At least until we get rid of him!'

They both looked around to see Pete tearing the van from his leg and throwing it effortlessly aside. He stared at them, unable to cross the water. Then he noticed a bridge on the northern side, and ran for it.

'We don't have much time,' said Toby, standing with

his hands up. 'He's absorbing energy, so every time we hit him, he grows bigger and stronger.'

'So we've got to stop hitting him? Can we trap him somehow?'

'I've tried that. When he grows bigger he can't fly and that's the only thing saving us right now.'

'Why should I trust you? Especially after what you did to me in Greece. I spent a whole day stuck on Easter Island! Do you know where that is? It's in the middle of nowhere!'

'I'm sorry!' shouted Toby, not quite believing that he was apologizing to the villain. 'But you were trying to mug me! Look we don't have time to stand around arguing, can we run and argue?'

Jen scowled, but they both ran through the trees as fast as they could.

'Don't try any tricks on me like that, or I *will* shoot you in the head,' warned Jen.

'Promise,' said Toby as sincerely as he could. He was already trying to figure out how to snatch the artefact away from her once they had given Pete the slip. 'I'd rather you have it than Pete.'

'Then that's something we both agree on.' She gave Toby a quizzical glance. 'Who'd have thought two enemies could agree on something like that?'

'Especially when one of them is on the run from his ex-best friend. Where are we?'

# Beat the Bullet

They left the trees and found themselves trampling across a perfectly manicured garden. It was situated on the edge of a courtyard that was overlooked by a large white building, the bulk of which was hidden by the garden.

Jen's face dropped. 'Aw . . . nuts!'

'What?'

Ten Japanese soldiers ran from the building. They were dressed in army camouflage uniforms and wielding deadly Howa Type 89 rifles. They screamed at Jen and Toby.

'This is the Imperial Palace! We're trespassing! I don't speak Japanese. What are they saying?'

Toby put his hands up. 'You can guess.'

'I haven't got time for this!'

The soldiers hesitated at the sight of the two innocent looking tourists.

'Power fist!' yelled Jen, startling the guards who all exchanged glances. Once again her headset glowed. She made a subtle sweeping gesture—and a telekinetic force blew three of the men to the ground.

'Run!' she yelled.

Toby heard gunfire erupt behind them and tree trunks ahead of them splintered. He summoned an ice wall, which stopped one wave of bullets, but was soon destroyed. It bought them enough time to round the corner—

Straight into a high wall topped with razor wire. Toby leapt effortlessly on top, squashing the wire underfoot. Jen hesitated below.

'I'm stuck!'

'Throw up your bag and I'll lift you over.'

Jen's eyes narrowed. 'You cheating little—'

The soldiers rounded the corner—at the same time Pete burst from the trees. He roared in fury. 'The artefact is mine!'

The soldiers wheeled around, firing on the monster.

'No!' screamed Toby.

But it was too late. Every bullet increased Pete's size. He twisted and turned as his joints expanded. The soldiers watched in shock, their ammunition running dry. Pete was six metres of unbridled rage. He tore up a tree and threw it at a section of troopers who were scattered like bowling pins.

Toby jumped down from the wall and grabbed Jen around the waist. She struggled.

'Get off me!'

'Shut up!'

Carrying Jen, he bounded over the wall as Pete uprooted another tree and used it to swat the remaining guards.

Toby and Jen found themselves in a car park. They ran as fast as they could. Ahead was another stretch of water, and Toby realized that the waterways were a large moat surrounding the Imperial Palace.

Jen extended her arms, once again creating the light bridge. She ran across. Toby followed—and his feet fell through the glowing bridge and he dropped into the water. He kicked his legs and fought his way to the surface.

'Help!' he spluttered.

Jen had reached the far side and the bridge vanished. She shrugged. 'I knew someone like you couldn't be trusted. If I had given you the bag back there you would have left me.'

'No I wouldn't! I saved you.'

'That makes up for dumping me on Easter Island.'

The wall exploded in a shower of masonry as Pete blasted his way through.

Jen winked at Toby. 'Keep him busy for me, shrimp.' Then she ran away across a broad parade ground, towards a busy road that lay beyond the palace gates.

Pete thundered towards Toby. He was so big that Toby could feel the vibrations in the water. There was no way Toby could out-swim him, so he dived downwards.

Toby was blind as he descended. It felt as if seconds passed before he finally touched the bottom. He hoped that his plan would work. He tensed himself—

Pete reached the water where Toby had been. He

jumped into the moat, kicking up a colossal wave of water. The water only came to his waist. He reached a hand in to where he thought Toby would be.

Toby exploded out of the moat and into the car park, avoiding Pete's grasp. In the distance, Jen was disappearing over the palace gates. Pete waded through the moat as more palace guards appeared. Gunshots peppered the water, distracting Pete.

It took Toby four bounds to cross the expansive grounds and leap over the palace gate. He looked at his scanner: Jen was close. Luckily the Foundation had made the device properly waterproof. The same couldn't be said for his pistol; water still poured from the weapon.

There was no sign of Pete behind him, but Toby could hear continuing gunfire. Seconds later a pair of military helicopters roared overhead, no doubt heading for the giant palace intruder. *That should keep him busy*, thought Toby. He set off after Jen, unable to shake the feeling that somehow he was abandoning Pete. After everything they had been through it didn't seem right to leave his brother-in-arms behind.

Toby tried to force those thoughts away. Pete had left him on a sinking ship. In fact, Pete had caused the ship to sink. Pete had made his decision. Now Toby was left to fight on his own and the stakes were high. It wasn't only about freeing Emily from the clutches of Lord

# Beat the Bullet

Eon; it was about saving the world, yet again. Rather than make him feel inspired and special, that thought gave him a crushing feeling of loneliness.

Toby had come to a busy crossroads. Following the tracker signal, he turned left. He stopped outside a massive red-brick building. Tokyo Station. Jen had gone inside.

Toby followed. The station was packed with people. Toby stopped and swung the chrono-scanner around in a circle. Jen was so close it was difficult to lock on to exactly *where* she was in the crowd. He pushed forward to the ticket barrier in time to see Jen disappearing into a long sleek train as the doors slid closed.

Seconds later the train began to pull out of the station, precisely on time like all of Japan's public transport. But this was no ordinary train. This was the Japanese *Shinkansen*—one of the world famous bullet trains.

Toby watched as the impossibly sleek 500 Series Shinkansen glided from the station. He would have to act fast if he was going to board the 186 mph train without any major superpowers.

O I O I O I
O I O I O I I
O I O I O I
O I O I
O I

# Which Side Are You On?

Jen walked down the spacious aisle of the bullet train to her designated seat. She placed the backpack next to her, touching the Temporal Dilator fragment inside for reassurance.

She had made sure there were multiple plans in place for her escape. The bullet train was one of them. It was headed for Osaka on the western tip of Japan where her superiors would pick her up. She sat back and relaxed, gazing through the tall windows as the train started to pick up speed.

The JR 500 glided through the city like a predatory silver snake. The long tapering cockpit looked as though it belonged on a jet fighter. Each of the eight passenger cars moved under its own power, making the train the fastest and most expensive in the world.

Toby had leapt over the barrier and bounced to the

end of the platform in three long strides as the train cleared the station. He leapt wildly for the train, missing by a centimetre the twenty-five-kilovolt wires that ran overhead, and landing on the rear carriage. His sweat-slicked palms started to slide across the smooth body as it accelerated. He tried to find a handhold but there was nothing to grab except the pantograph that buzzed with the high-powered charge that it conducted from the overhead wires. Toby would be fried if he tried to grab hold of that, and no superpower he had would save him.

He slid backwards, towards the tracks—then he suddenly stopped moving. He must have some type of adhesive power. Toby breathed a sigh of relief. Now all he had to do was find a way into the train.

He scrambled onto the side of the Shinkansen, sticking to the smooth curved surface. He scuttled across several windows; fortunately the passengers were too busy reading or sleeping to notice him pass.

He reached a door and pulled on it. It didn't budge. Not for the first time he wondered what Kirby's thinking had been in equipping him with such a useless panoply of abilities.

He punched the glass—and immediately regretted it as his fingers broke. He gritted his teeth as they healed. Then he caught movement ahead—a white train was coming towards him, another bullet train, approaching *fast*.

# Which Side Are You On?

Toby drew his gun and fired at the glass. Nothing happened, except that more water dribbled from it. Toby didn't have time to complain. He fumbled for anything in his backpack that could help but because he was attached horizontally across the side of the train, half his gadgets fell out as he reached for them.

As the approaching train reached him, Toby flattened himself against the Shinkansen. There was barely enough clearance between the two trains, but Toby's ears popped from the violent change in air pressure and he felt himself being pulled off.

The unpleasant experience was over in seconds, but everything sounded muffled, as if he had water in his ears. The train continued picking up speed as they entered Tokyo's suburbs. They passed under several bridges, and Toby thought each one would decapitate him. He *had* to get inside the train.

In a fit of desperation he placed his hand over the window and let his ice shield cover the glass. The window cracked and Toby smashed his elbow into it. It broke into harmless pieces and he crawled through the narrow gap.

He found himself in an empty carriage. He smiled. Jen couldn't escape from a moving train. Retrieving the artefact would be easy.

He swept the scanner around. Jen was sitting ahead of him. Toby walked through two carriages before he saw the back of her head. She was sitting in the aisle seat with the backpack against the window. Toby sat in the spare seat across the aisle from her.

'Hello again,' he said.

Jen was startled to see him. Her hand instinctively grabbed the backpack. 'What are you doing here?'

'I thought you might be worried about me,' he said sarcastically.

'Why would I ever be worried about you?'

'Well, after I saved *your* life, I thought you might be worried about *mine*.'

'I'm not, and now we're even.'

'Actually I recall saving your life in Greece too.'

Jen looked away, she had forgotten about that.

'So why don't you hand the artefact over and then we'll call it even?'

'You stole the last one from me!'

'But you're still alive and in one piece. And you'll be alive for longer if we can activate the Temporal Dilator and use it to stop Eon from tearing a hole in time and space.'

Jen looked curiously at him. 'Why are you doing this?'

It was Toby's turn to look puzzled. 'Because I think saving the world is a good thing to do.'

'Do you really think your people are interested in that? Sure, they want to stop Lord Eon—we all want that, but at what price? Is it worth saving the world if your side is going to exploit Eon's powers for their own gain?'

'What do you mean?'

'Don't pretend you don't know. You lot are the same.'

Toby didn't want to admit ignorance, but his silence spoke volumes. Jen laughed, she was enjoying this.

'Oh, shrimp, you really *are* clueless!' Toby scowled at her, but she ignored him. 'Look, the Dilator is thousands of years old; so is Lord Eon. It was created in the days of real heroes, crafted from a meteor that broke up when it entered the earth's atmosphere. It doesn't defeat Eon, it neutralizes his power by *absorbing* his chronons.'

'There's a big difference between neutralizing it and exploiting it.'

'Not really. If it sucks up the chronons that give Eon his power then where do you think they're stored?'

The answer was obvious. 'In the artefact itself.'

'Bull's-eye, shrimp. And that's why Lord Eon can't touch them himself. They would drain his power. He doesn't want the parts of the Temporal Dilator to put the machine together, he wants them destroyed! That's why the old heroes scattered the pieces. They were too valuable to destroy in case Eon or any other Temporal raider ever threatened the world again. But that's not enough for your side. They want to synthesize Eon's powers for their own benefit. Now that Eon is loose again, everybody is scrambling to retrieve the Temporal Dilator for themselves. Your lot included.'

'But you know your side will just abuse that power too?'

Jen laughed. 'Sure, because that's what we do, right?'

'That's why I'm taking it from you, so don't make a scene. There are other passengers on the train and there is no need for them to get hurt.'

'Was that a threat?' asked Jen, her eyes narrowing. 'Is it going to be the cruise ship all over again?'

'That wasn't my fault!'

'Sure it wasn't. If you're thinking of taking hostages, that's low. Even for a two . . . ' She trailed off. 'Look behind you.'

It was Toby's turn to laugh. 'Oh come on! You don't seriously expect that to work on me, do you? I wasn't born yesterday!'

A sound like a giant hammer slamming an equally huge anvil suddenly rang through the train. Passengers screamed as the train rocked on its tracks.

Toby whirled round to witness a jagged hole appearing in the side of the carriage. The wind blasted in and passengers were sucked from their seats.

Pete was flying alongside the train—now back to his normal size. His eyes were glowing molten red from the laser vision that had carved the side off the train. He swooped inside, landing on the seats. Screaming passengers fled from the carriage.

'Give me the Dilator and things don't have to get messy.'

'No way!' shouted Jen and Toby in unison.

Blue flames erupted around Pete's hands as he nodded at Jen. 'You were quick replacing us with a new little super team.'

'I'm not working with her!' said Toby.

'Looks like it to me. Last chance.'

Anger flushed through Toby. He was already irritated that the Foundation hadn't trusted him enough to explain the truth behind his mission. Perhaps they thought he wouldn't approve of them synthesizing Eon's powers? And on top of that he was furious that his friendships had been torn apart—Emily captured, Lorna . . . well, she could be anywhere, and Pete turned to the dark side.

He felt his hands tingle, a familiar sign that an attack power was brewing. He was hit by a sudden wave of hope. Kirby had been adamant that he wouldn't load Toby with any assault capabilities, but in his haste to get him out of the Foundation he must have done so. But why didn't he tell him?

Pete jumped off the seat and walked down the aisle. 'I'm not waiting. Give me the artefact and you both walk out of here. I know you don't have any attack powers, Tobe. You would have shot me ages ago.'

Toby raised his hands and stood up. He motioned for Jen to do so. 'You're right, Pete. But you do know that Lord Eon will kill you when you deliver the last piece of the Temporal Dilator?'

'That's not your problem. *I'm* your problem.'

'You know, Pete, every time you have powers you get cocky. That's your weakness.'

Pete didn't see Toby's hands move—but a sizzling cord of energy whipped out and slashed him across the face. Pete felt his skin burn and he staggered backwards.

'Run!' shouted Toby. He had been hoping for an electrical attack or a fireball, but the energy whip that snaked from his fingers served the purpose. He pushed Jen down the carriage.

They ran through the automatic door between carriages.

'He's coming!' warned Jen.

Pete was already charging down the aisle. He'd absorbed Toby's attack and was centimetres bigger. The automatic doors opened as he approached.

'Duck!' yelled Jen.

Toby instinctively crouched before he realized what Jen intended. 'No! It'll only make him—'

BAM! Her energy blast shattered the glass doors and

peeled open the end of the carriage like a sardine tin. It was so intense that Pete was thrown backwards.

' . . . bigger,' finished Toby lamely. 'That's not a lot of help.'

'I didn't see you suggest anything better! Besides, I thought it was a rather good idea. Now he can't fly.'

'So?'

Jen pointed back at Pete. The carriages were drifting apart. Her blast had destroyed the coupling. Pete was in the section being pulled by the head of the train and even though every carriage was propelled under its own power, the gap was slowly widening. Despite himself Toby was impressed.

'Now let's go,' said Jen as she ran away. Toby scrambled to his feet and quickly followed. They had reached the second carriage before he looked back. The distance between the two halves of the train was half a carriage length—but Pete was taking a running jump.

They ran into the next corridor as Pete leapt—making it by the skin of his teeth. He balanced on the edge, a step away from falling under the train.

Jen and Toby had already increased their lead into yet another carriage.

'We're at the back of the train!' shouted Jen. 'What are we going to do?'

Toby looked around for a solution, but without a

way of trapping Pete there was little they could do except keep running.

'Outside!' he shouted.

'Are you crazy?'

Toby tried to open the door, but the safety lock held it firmly in place while they were moving. 'Can you open this?'

He stood back as Jen blasted the door from its runners.

'Follow me!' Toby scuttled along the side of the train, his powers keeping him attached.

'I can't do that!' shouted Jen over the wind.

'Reach out! I'll pull you up.'

Jen reached out and gripped his hand—and Toby saw his chance to snatch the Dilator. With his feet sticking him to the side of the train, he reached out his other hand and pulled the backpack off Jen's shoulder.

'Hey! You creep!'

Toby released her hand. 'Sorry. But you'd do the same.'

Jen stood in the open doorway, battered by the wind, arms akimbo—as Pete tackled her to the floor. She screamed as they smashed through the seats.

Toby scuttled on top of the train, keeping his head low to avoid the overhead cables. He checked the Dilator was in Jen's pack before securing it in his own; he wouldn't put it past her to have led him on a wild goose chase. But it was there. All he had to do was call for a ride home.

Beneath him an explosion ripped through the windows either side of the carriage. He guessed that Jen was being pummelled. To his surprise he felt ashamed at leaving her alone to face Pete. His old friend was out of control, capable of *anything*. Even murder.

Toby tried to ignore his feelings. She was a villain and deserved what she got. The Council of Evil could save her. He scampered to the edge of the train and hit the video call button. Seconds later Kirby answered.

'Do you have it?'

'Yes, and I need to get out of here pronto!'

'We're on our way.' The signal cut at the same time that the entire carriage lurched and he heard Jen scream.

Toby felt low. He had abandoned a girl to get beaten up by Pete. Even if she was a villain . . . Toby slapped his forehead.

'Tobe, you muppet!' It didn't help shake the feeling of guilt. He sighed; being a hero was about doing the right thing, even if that meant saving the bad guys.

'I'm going to regret this,' he mumbled as he swung through the broken window.

Jen was bleeding and badly bruised. Pete was towering over her, two and a half metres tall, curved talons extending from his fingernails like tiger's claws. From the slash marks across Jen's chest he had already attacked her with them.

'Pete, you coward! Hitting a girl while she's down?'

'Who's down?' snarled Jen, spitting out blood.

Toby ignored her. 'I thought you wanted the artefact. I have it right here.' He patted his backpack.

Pete looked confused. 'I thought she had it?'

'I told you I didn't!' screamed Jen.

For a second Pete looked remorseful. Then he turned on Toby. 'So you let her take all the punishment while you ran? I should kill you right now!'

'But you won't. You're the sad, pathetic loser you've always been. The kid who was always beaten up because he wouldn't fight back.'

'I'll fight back now. I'll fight *anyone*. Especially you. You never stood up for me at school!' They both knew that wasn't true, Toby had always tried to watch his friend's back, but now didn't seem the time to correct him. 'You never wanted me to access Hero.com, you never wanted me to have any control or power of my own. It all had to come though you!'

The hatred in Pete's voice shocked Toby. He realized that there was nothing he could say or do. They were bitter enemies now, whether Toby liked it or not.

'I don't need you any more. I don't need you or Hero.com. I have my own powers. My own friends.'

'And what will you do when they run out? You'll just

be that kid again, the one everybody picks on.' Toby
instantly regretted saying that. 'But there's still time for
you to get help. Come back with me.'

'Forget it. There's nothing you can say to change my
mind.'

'I bet Emily could.'

Pete hesitated, and then regained his composure.
'Maybe I can persuade her to join Villain.net. The
Council have some great perks. It would prevent you
from using her too.'

'So that's who you've sided with?'

'I'm weighing up my options. You see, for once, I
have a choice.'

'Do you really think the Council will exist after Lord
Eon destroys the Dilator, the only thing that can stop
him? He's out for himself. He's going to bring both
sides down!'

'I know that now. That's why he's not going to get it.'

Toby blinked in surprise. 'Then who . . . ?'

'That piece of the Dilator is going to the Council of
Evil, and they will reward me for it! A real reward, not
like the pat on the back the Foundation gives you.'

Pete's betrayal hurt Toby more than any of their pre-
vious arguments. He'd actually gone to the dark side.
'Mate, when this is over and Eon is back in whatever
pit they throw him in, I'm going to come after you. I'm
going to come after you and bring the Council down

around your head. The whole Foundation will back me.'

Jen was looking confused. 'What are you talking about?'

Toby looked at her—and a question popped into his mind. 'Why are you fighting him? You two are on the same side!'

He started backing away, but the confused look on Jen's face made him stop. 'What!?' Before Toby could react the world *whip-whapped* around them. All three staggered as they each experienced their own déjà vu.

'*Eon's* here!' growled Pete.

They looked around—but couldn't see the villain.

'Show yourself!' shouted Toby, feeling braver than he felt. A colossal force hit the carriage. Everybody was thrown to the ground as the train lurched off the track.

'Hold on to something!' screamed Jen as they were flung around like clothes in a washing machine.

The train rolled over-and-over, finally coming to a rest in a paddy field.

Fire ripped through the engines and in seconds the carriages were alight. Pete punched a hole in the roof of a carriage and staggered out, followed moments later by Toby and Jen.

'Everyone OK?' asked Toby, out of habit.

'Give me the piece.'

# Which Side Are You On?

'No!' Toby's energy whip uncoiled from his fingers towards Pete.

Despite his bulky size and his cyan, disintegrating skin, Pete managed to look innocent. 'I didn't say that.'

'Do I have to ask again?' said the voice.

They all spun round to see Lord Eon standing in the field. He looked out of place: overly tall, in his perfect three-piece suit, hovering centimetres above the muddy field. He extended his hand, not flinching as one of the carriages exploded.

'You're not having it, Eon,' said Toby defiantly. Even though he'd been in tighter spots than this he still felt scared. He'd always had the back-up of his friends before. Now he was unsure whose support he did have.

'Then I shall take it from you, boy.'

'I don't believe you can. If you touch it, it will absorb your power. Maybe I should throw it to you, and we can play catch?' Toby slid the backpack off his shoulder and pretended to throw it. *That* made Eon flinch.

Eon stared at Toby as if he was something he'd just found on the bottom of his shoe. 'I would kill you all right now. But you still have a service to perform.'

'Go to hell!' said Pete. 'I'm not working for you any more. I know you're using me and that doesn't happen from now on. You're his enemy, and you're my enemy—two against one. Good odds.' Pete stood next to Toby.

Toby glanced at his ex-friend and got the faintest of nods in support. Jen surprised him by standing alongside too.

'Make it three,' she said.

Eon didn't look perturbed. 'For years I festered on Diablo Island, unable to use my gifts. However, there was one power I had that they couldn't strip away.' He tapped his temple. 'The power of thought, the power of imagination, the power to plan my own escape.'

Toby was confused. '*Plan* your escape? But you got out when they were trying to spring Viral. It was an accident.'

'I got out, because I reasoned what events would have to occur in the *future* to allow my escape now. We stand at the head of time. Before us lies the unknown. Even I cannot travel beyond *the moment*. I can merely guess what it will be. But the past is a complex thing. What we do *now* influences it.'

'Two things,' grunted Pete. 'You've lost me. And I don't care.'

'Oh, you will. In fact, in a way you already *have*. If only you knew the correct historical records to look at.'

Lord Eon raised his hands and closed his eyes. Pete and Jen fired their powers at exactly the same time—but that didn't prevent the world from warping.

Toby saw Jen reach out to grab him—and they were instantaneously in another place . . . and another time.

# Déjà vu

Toby thought that he had grown used to the sickening feeling of teleporting, but the waves of nausea hit him hard. Pete was on his hands and knees retching. The teleport must have scrambled Pete's powers because he was now back to his normal size. Toby looked around— Jen was nowhere to be seen. It looked as if Eon had only teleported the pair of them.

Toby took off his backpack and searched through it. The Temporal Dilator piece was missing! He recalled the final few seconds as Jen had reached for him. She hadn't been trying to save him; she had been saving the Temporal Dilator. Part of him felt angry, but another part of him hoped that she had taken it beyond Eon's reach. But questions remained. Why was she fighting Pete if he had switched allegiances from Eon to the Council? But the most important question at the moment was *where* were they?

The spluttering noise of a petrol engine got his attention. He turned slowly round, taking in their surroundings. There was a broad airstrip behind him, carved from the dense surrounding jungle.

'My head feels like it has been hit by a hammer,' said Pete as he climbed to his feet. 'Where are we?'

'I think the better question is *when* are we?'

Pete followed Toby's gaze. 'Wow!' he exclaimed.

Three bombers lined the runway, gleaming new in the hot noon sun. What was immediately obvious was that instead of jet engines, they had propellers on each wing.

'Lancaster bombers,' said Pete in awe. The throaty sound of petrol engines came from a pair of Spitfires that were accelerating up the runway.

'I have a very bad feeling about this,' said Toby.

'Tobe, look.'

A pair of soldiers marched across the runway, wooden-stocked M1903 Springfield rifles pointed menacingly at them. The soldiers wore the deep green American uniforms that both boys had seen in World War Two films.

'Hold it right there, boys!' shouted a sergeant in a southern drawl. 'You know you're trespassin'?'

'Why has Eon brought us here?' whispered Toby as he raised his hands.

'I don't know. To get us out of the way? Why don't we just blast these jokers?'

'Let's find out where we are first.'

# Déjà vu

The sergeant studied them with deep mistrust. The private behind him nervously kept the gun trained on them. He obviously thought they were a threat.

'What're you kids doin' all the way out here? You spyin' on us?'

'No, sir,' said Toby nervously. He might have powers to get out of the situation, but he knew he couldn't dodge a bullet at short range.

Pete lowered his hands and took a step forward. The jittery private took several paces back, raising the gun higher.

'Don't wave guns at us. We're supers.'

Toby was impressed with the confidence in Pete's voice.

'I told ya, Sarge!' squeaked the private.

'Shut up, Private!' The sergeant motioned his gun towards the buildings on the other side of the airfield. 'Then you won't mind coming with us, will ya?'

Pete shrugged casually. 'Whatever. But don't think for a second that those guns can hurt us.'

The soldiers led them to a knot of wooden huts. Toby's stomach was churning, both from nervousness and the unexpected jump through time. He was amazed how Pete was taking it all in his stride. Normally Pete would be the nervous one, but his expression and gait showed that he was brimming with confidence. Toby wondered if there was such a superpower as *confidence*, because Pete had it in abundance. As much as he hated to admit it, joining the Council of Evil had done Pete a world of good.

'Wait here,' ordered the sergeant. He entered a hut, leaving the nervous private watching them.

'You really supers? Or you yanking my chain?' he asked in a trembling voice.

Pete smiled and lifted his hand. Sparks danced across his fingers. The private was mesmerized.

'Wow! Someday I gotta get me some of them!'

'Some day you will be able to,' muttered Toby.

The sergeant appeared at the door and whistled for their attention. He beckoned them inside with his finger.

A large map of the immediate area was laid on a central table. Pins and metal markers displayed positions of troops and equipment. The corner of the room was dominated by bulky radio and radar equipment. Three operators sat with their backs to the boys, listening to radio chatter. A young man stood over them, talking animatedly. Then he turned round and studied the boys.

Toby and Pete gasped—they recognized him straight away. It was Eric Kirby. He looked decades younger and wasn't walking with a cane, but the gleam in his eyes was unmistakable. He wore a white, armoured body-suit with a red 'CC' logo on his chest. Bright red belt, boots, and a cape finished off the clichèd uniform. He looked every bit the dated superhero.

Kirby studied the boys curiously, idly twisting a ring on his left index finger. Toby recognized it as an early incarnation of the Foundation logo.

'So you boys claim to be supers?'

'Eric Kirby!' exclaimed Pete.

Kirby looked at him suspiciously. 'How do you know my name? I'm Commander Courage!'

Toby interjected; it didn't feel right to tell Kirby about the future. 'Your exploits are legendary to all Downloaders.'

Kirby frowned. 'What's a Downloader?'

Toby mentally kicked himself. Of course, there was no Internet now. In fact the computers of the age were nothing more than basic valve and resistor contraptions. 'It's what we call supers where we come from,' he said lamely.

'We've got powers all right,' said Pete, displaying the flickering sparks between his fingers again.

'Indeed you have. But the question is, which side are you fighting for?'

Toby glanced at Pete, willing him not to tell the truth. Luckily Pete was thinking ahead.

'On the Allies' side, of course.'

'And why are you here?'

Toby and Pete exchanged looks. Toby improvised.

'We were teleported in from HQ. I'm Toby and this is my fr-friend, Pete.'

'I heard the bang, sir,' said the private. 'And I saw 'em appear across the runway.'

Kirby nodded. 'Good, and in the nick of time. Although I was hoping for Primes a *little older*. But unfortunately this war is turning out to be increasingly fought by the young.' With a flick of the hand, Kirby dismissed the two soldiers. 'You may leave us.' He looked critically at the boys' clothes. 'I don't think much of your uniforms.'

Pete looked at his stylish black jumpsuit and shrugged. Toby was in his jeans and trainers, and looked perfectly normal. It seemed old people didn't have taste even when they were young.

'Where exactly are we?' asked Toby. Kirby looked at him with a trace of suspicion. 'HQ were thin on the details,' Toby added with a shrug, hoping that he sounded genuine.

'Mexico.'

Pete and Toby had been here a little over a month ago. Then a gang of supervillains had kidnapped Pete. Toby, Lorna, and Emily had rescued him. That experience was the start of Pete's villainous switch.

'Worm!' growled Pete, clenching his fists so hard that flickers of lightning arced down to the floor.

'I'm glad they briefed you about some of the mission

then. The Axis forces haven't reached these shores yet, although our regular troops are patrolling the coasts for secret submarine refuelling depots. However, there are contingents of villains who are using the conflict for their own nefarious purposes. Worm has set up base somewhere in the jungle and is assembling his forces. He is waiting for the war to weaken the world enough for him to take control. It's our job to find him and put a stop to it.'

A wailing klaxon sounded from outside, and seconds later gunfire cracked through the air.

'Or him to find us!' finished Kirby as he ran over to the radar screens.

'Sir, we have ten incoming targets below one angel!'

Kirby dashed for the door. 'Come on, boys, time to prove you can fight!'

Outside, a platoon of soldiers was running across the runway. An anti-aircraft gun spun on its fixed pedestal and fired flak into the air. The shells exploded in the sky with dull POM-POM sounds.

Kirby, Pete, and Toby looked up at the sky, searching for the enemy.

'Can you fly?' asked Kirby.

'Not today,' shouted Toby. Kirby gave him a curious look, and Toby realized how sarcastic his reply had sounded in a time when powers couldn't be chosen.

Pete hovered in the air. 'I can.'

Kirby closed his eyes and swept his palm across the jungle. He fixed on one point, using his second sight to see beyond the trees. 'There! Aerial henchmen!'

Seconds later Worm's first wave of men flew over the tree line. They wore green one-piece uniforms and each had a set of bi-plane wings strapped to his back, powered by four tiny propellers. Pete laughed, they looked so out of date. The sky-troopers carried small multi-barrelled Gatling guns, which they unleashed with deadly force. He stopped laughing—a bullet was a bullet.

Pete flew straight for the lead thug, out-racing the trail of Gatling fire as the man tried to shoot him down. Pete was quicker and more nimble than the primitive flier. He corkscrewed around so he was above the man—and unleashed his blue fire. The wood and canvas flight-pack was vaporized and the man fell to earth with a wail. Pete laughed and flew to the next man.

Kirby's troops scattered as the dirt was pocked with heavy gunfire. Without superpowers, the aerial assault was lethal, killing one man on the ground. Kirby bounced across the open spaces with balletic grace, appearing amongst groups of his soldiers so he could protect them from the barrage by casting his energy-shield around them.

Grounded, Toby felt useless as the sky-troopers soared overhead. One swooped low, strafing him. He summoned his ice shield to absorb the bullets, while his other hand lashed out with the crackling light-whip. The coiling whip snaked around the man's leg, burning into his skin. As the plasma filament grew taut it tethered the man who—with nowhere to go—was forced into a nosedive, crashing head-first through the roof of a building.

Pete was easily dispatching the circling fliers, but he was moving too leisurely and the enemy had managed to injure several soldiers below. Toby lashed the whip out again, severing the wing of a passing flier. The henchman spiralled into the trees.

'Toby! I sense Worm is approaching! Be ready!' yelled Kirby from across the airfield.

Toby looked around, wondering where the attack would come from. Then the ground shook and a sleek bronze machine erupted from the earth—it was Worm's prize possession, the Nematode. An opening at the front gnashed through the ground, and shredded through a Lancaster bomber parked above it. Two dome windows on the front of the machine gave it an insect-like appearance, and inside Toby could see the familiar bald, blunt head of his old enemy.

Toby sprinted towards the vehicle, unsure how he could stop it. Pete had seen Worm's arrival as he dispatched the last of the fliers. With a snarl of rage, he swooped low.

Bullets ricocheted from the Nematode's hull as the circling soldiers opened fire. Pete unleashed a powerful blast that rocked the machine and caught the fuel tank of a parked Lancaster, causing it to explode in a cloud of black smoke.

A hatch on top of the Nematode slid open and its sonic cannon rotated out on a clockwork assembly. The weapon was covered in valves and wires and resembled an elongated bullhorn. It swivelled towards Pete and a bass-heavy sound-wave shot out and slammed into him. He was flung backwards, his mass increasing as he absorbed the energy—but his flight powers gave up. Pete plummeted to the tarmac below.

A pair of Spitfires circled the area, machine guns chattering. Toby was forced to leap aside as their enfilade tore the ground next to him and smashed into the Nematode.

The sonic cannon whirled round, blasting one of the Spitfires from the air. Toby ran in front of the Nematode as it crawled forward. He saw Worm inside staring straight at him. Toby uncurled his energy whip and held his ground. It was enough of a distraction for Worm to miss the second Spitfire with his sonic cannon.

Worm made a cut-throat gesture at Toby and angled the cannon straight down at him. Toby shot his ice blast across the canopy window, frosting it. Then he leapt aside as the sonic weapon pummelled the ground where he had been standing seconds before.

Unable to see, Worm wildly spun the cannon and fired. Kirby protected a group of soldiers by deflecting several shots with his shield. Pete blasted the flanks of the machine with everything he had. His face was twisted with rage.

The Nematode fuselage started to buckle and smoke as the remaining Spitfire roared in, pummelling the weak spot.

Worm made a tactical retreat. Unable to see his enemy, he angled the Nematode into the ground and swiftly dug through the limestone, vanishing like a shark under water. The earth the machine scooped from the front was passed through the Nematode and ejected at the back, blocking his escape route.

Pete screamed in fury, continuing to shoot at the ground. Toby slowly approached. 'Pete! Whoa, calm down. He's gone.'

Pete stopped, but the look of hatred remained on his face. 'I'm going to *kill* him.'

This time Toby didn't doubt his sincerity. 'He's gone, Pete.'

'He destroyed my home. He kidnapped me and he put me in a cryogenic freeze. If it wasn't for him I wouldn't have been in that coma!'

Toby didn't know what to say. Pete was overlooking

the role Worm's conspirators had played: Basilisk, Trojan, and Viral. However, in a way he was right. Without Worm in that equation Basilisk would have been unable to attack the Foundation and perhaps Pete would not have changed. And maybe that would mean they wouldn't be standing here . . .

Toby's head hurt. Kirby—the old Kirby—had explained the problems with time paradoxes. He had also said they were impossible.

'Pete, you can't kill him here.'

'Why not?'

Toby moved closer, he didn't want Kirby to overhear. 'Because we already met him in the future—our present,' he corrected himself.

'But if I kill him now then none of that would have happened to us.'

'Exactly. It's impossible. Look, Kirby told me how this works. You can't change the past. This has already *happened*!'

'That's impossible,' snarled Pete. 'Because we would have had to have been stuck here in the nineteen forties already . . .'

Pete trailed off, trying to work it out.

Toby recalled when he had first seen Worm. The villains had been breaking Viral out of Diablo Island and Worm had hesitated when he saw Toby. It was as if he recognized him. Now Toby knew why.

# Déjà vu

'We're here now,' said Toby patiently. 'It doesn't matter that, for us, this is our present. To the rest of the world everything we do here has already occurred. It's history. History we so happen to be in.'

'What's to stop me shoving my hand in his face and blasting a fireball down his gob?' pressed Pete.

'Because if you were in a position to do it, it would have already happened! Look, you can't go back in time and stop wars or save people from dying because you simply *were not there to begin with*. You might have been standing right next to the person you wanted to save, or in the next street, but *something* stopped you from saving them.'

Pete wasn't buying the explanation. He'd seen too many films where the space-time continuum had been altered. He'd rather believe the fiction than facts. He glared at Toby.

'See what you do? You always try and take control,' he snapped.

'What are you talking about?'

'You're telling me right now what I can and cannot do.'

'Because it's impossible!'

'Flying is supposed to be impossible, but I can still do it.'

Toby tried to calm him down. 'Pete, listen—'

'No, you listen. The only reason I haven't punched

your face through is because I don't want to be stuck back here like an antique. I'm only working with you until we get back home, and then if I see your face in my business you're in trouble.'

'What happened back in Japan? We were side-by-side then. Back to being mates.'

'An alliance formed only to fight Eon. After that, you and the brat girl would have been next.'

Toby was intimidated. He nodded, for the first time in his life feeling what it was like to be bullied. He knew there was no way he could fight Pete without access to more superpowers. He glanced at his phone; not surprisingly there was no signal. For once he couldn't blame his service provider—they wouldn't exist for another fifty years.

Kirby ran over to them as fire crews tackled the blazes around the camp. 'Are you chaps OK?' Toby nodded. Kirby was beaming. 'You were both impressive. That was a very brave thing to do, standing up to the Nematode like that.' The last comment was aimed at Toby. Pete rolled his eyes.

'So now what? Where is he?' snapped Pete.

Kirby looked at the two boys. He could feel the tension between them. 'Our practical forces have taken quite a hit here. It's difficult to get replacements sent over. At this rate we'll never find Worm's base.'

# Déjà vu

'Can't you use your second-sight power?' asked Toby.

'Alas, no. Worm has found a way to block it, that's why I couldn't sense the attack until they were upon us. We have to rely on solid manpower to track him down.'

'I know where he is,' said Pete quietly.

Kirby looked at him questioningly. Toby closed his eyes. Of course they knew. In the future his dad had discovered the ruins of Worm's secret base. In the future they had already been there . . .

The three supers pushed their way through the dense foliage, and for Toby it brought back memories of a time when he had been determined to save Pete. He was with his friend again but knew that Pete would no longer return the favour and save Toby's life. Toby brooded on how quickly friendships can fall apart.

'We're close,' said Pete. He had flown ahead to reconnoitre the jungle and had found the twin Mayan pyramids where Worm had his base. One of them had an array of antennas poking from the flat top.

Kirby brushed foliage aside, and then froze. 'Keep quiet,' he whispered. 'There are guards everywhere.'

The boys peeked between the branches. Sure enough the area between the jungle and the pyramid was crawling with Worm's alert henchmen. The area wasn't as overgrown as Toby had remembered, and a clear path now ran between the two pyramids.

A door led into the nearest structure, a metal 'S' attached to it. Toby had originally thought it was a snake, rather than a depiction of a worm. A worm was less impressive.

'We need to storm the building through that door.'

Toby shook his head. 'No. Once through there it's a spiralling corridor all the way up. If we can't do it stealthily then we'd end up battling every step of the way.'

'How could you possibly know that?'

Toby blushed and looked away, mumbling, 'It's an ability of mine.'

He looked up the structure's steep stepped sides. When he was last here the top level had looked solid but had been camouflaged with a holographic wall. That technology did not yet exist, and he could see that a panoramic window had been installed across the wall instead.

'We can enter through the top though.'

'But we'd still have to get past the guards,' said Kirby thoughtfully. 'We'd have to create a distraction to lure them away. Pete, perhaps you could . . . Pete?'

They both looked around. Pete had vanished. Toby looked back at the pyramid and saw Pete had flown to the top, completely unseen by the guards.

# Déjà vu

'He can't do it on his own!' exclaimed Kirby. 'We still need a diversion.'

Pete landed on top of the pyramid. He didn't care what Toby said, he was going to kill Worm. His hatred for Worm was matched only by his desire for self-preservation. He knew that even if he could turn back time, the animosity he felt for Toby was not going to go away, but at the very least he could still save his friendship with Emily.

And if he had to sacrifice others for that goal, so be it.

Toby watched Pete take aim directly at him. Even from this distance he could see the fierce expression on Pete's face and he knew exactly what Pete was going to do.

'I think *we* are the diversion.'

Pete blasted the trees in front of Toby and Kirby. Kirby's shield protected them both from the splinters of wood that floored several of the guards. They were thrown onto their backs—and thirty well-trained soldiers aimed their guns straight at them.

\* \* \*

Exposing his 'friends' to the enemy was a small price to pay to save himself. Besides, if he could change the future they would never know what he had done!

Pete watched as the guards scrambled into action below. They would be distracted enough not to see Pete punch through the panoramic window and leap inside Worm's lair.

The diminutive supervillain was at the controls of the large cryogenic chamber that Pete had been trapped in over a month ago—or almost seven decades in the future depending on which way you counted.

Worm spun around in alarm—his eyes widening at the sight of the blue-faced, cracked-skinned, muscular boy in front of him. He was a far cry from the gawky bespectacled kid Worm would meet in the future. No wonder he wouldn't recognize him.

'Who are you?' he snapped.

Pete didn't reply. He summoned a fist of fire and hurled it at Worm.

Kirby's shield shimmered in the air as thirty guns blazed simultaneously. Under such an onslaught the shield was beginning to crackle and fade.

'Shoot them with something!'

'I don't have anything!' Toby rummaged in his bag and pulled out the only three gadgets that hadn't fallen out when he'd been clinging to the side of the train. He recognized one. 'Hold on to something!'

He selected a shiny metal sphere with a row of LEDs around the circumference. He thumbed a recessed trigger and watched as the lights illuminated in a domino effect. He hurled the ball into the centre of the mob and threw both hands around a tree trunk.

The sphere exploded with a very un-dramatic pop. The thirty guards suddenly froze in place. Toby stood up with a satisfied grin. Kirby was looking at him with admiration.

'What was that contraption?'

'Paralysis bomb. These guys won't be moving for hours.'

'How does it work?'

Toby knew he shouldn't give too much away as the technology was still decades from being discovered. 'Oh, you know. It's complicated,' he mumbled. 'Let me keep *some* of my secrets. Now let's stop Pete before things get really messy!'

The moment he said that a fireball erupted from the top of the pyramid and Worm rolled down the building's stepped side, crying out as he bounced against it. Halfway down his body crumbled into dust and poured the rest of the way down the structure, only to reform into Worm at the bottom of the steps, lying flat on his face and dazed from the pummelling that Pete had given him. One of Worm's powers enabled him to do that so that he could travel through the dirt. It was the same power Toby had been able to use in Greece. How had the Foundation managed to steal that from the villain?

'Get him before he tries to escape!' yelled Kirby as he rushed forward.

'He won't go anywhere,' said Toby confidently. He remembered that, without the Nematode, Worm was unable to travel through the solid limestone that made up most of the Yucatan Peninsula they now stood on. That's one of the reasons the pyramid had made a perfect prison for Worm.

Toby felt a thrill when he realized that history was unfolding around him. He knew that Kirby would imprison Worm in his own cryogenics machine inside the pyramid. He also knew that something terrible would befall Kirby, wiping his memory of all these events.

Pete landed in front of them. 'Let me at him!'

'Not a chance! You can't change history! Will you listen to me?'

Pete swatted his hand like he would a fly—and Toby felt the psychokinetic blast slam into his chest and suck the breath from him. He was lifted into the air and walloped against a tree. But he didn't fall. Pete maintained the power and held Toby above the ground.

# Déjà vu

'You never know when to shut up, do you? Maybe I should shove *you* in the cryo-chamber and see how you like having your blood frozen?'

Kirby looked between the two of them. 'What is going on here? I thought you were friends?'

'Some things are beyond friendship,' growled Pete and, with a twist of his hand, he flung Toby repeatedly into the side of the pyramid. The pain was overwhelming and Toby could feel his regeneration powers constantly healing bones that were broken again seconds later. It was the internal bleeding that would kill him as his powers fought to save him.

'Stop it!' yelled Kirby.

'Or what?' shouted Pete. 'I've had enough of you and your stupid Foundation! Using people like me to download your powers to do your dirty work because you Primes are afraid of getting hurt. You put our lives on the line and give nothing in return!'

Kirby didn't have a clue what Pete was venting about. It would be many more years before the Internet existed, let alone the technology to synthesize powers and download them through Hero.com. It was something that would surface in Kirby's subconscious many years later. Without realizing it, Pete had given the superhero the spark that would create the very thing he was complaining about.

Pete stopped pounding Toby against the wall. Toby

remained suspended in the air, limp and close to blacking out. He could just see Pete through the blood oozing from his scalp. He could feel his abilities fighting to regenerate his shattered body. The chain of events that occurred next happened so fast that Toby had trouble following them.

Pete used his free hand to shoot at Worm. The close proximity should have meant certain death for the villain but—

Kirby leapt in front of his prisoner. The fierce energy blast slammed directly into him. Toby watched in horror as the blast threw Kirby's body across the clearing, his ultra-white uniform black and smouldering as he crumbled, unmoving, to the ground.

Pete was so shocked that he had just attacked the head of the Hero Foundation that he forgot about holding Toby up. Toby collapsed at the foot of the pyramid.

When Toby sat upright he saw that Worm was on all-fours, scrambling away from Pete who was stalking him. The bloodlust was evident in Pete's eyes and cobalt fire dripped from his hands.

'Please spare me!' whined Worm.

Toby didn't have the powers to stop Pete—but he had the gadgets. He pulled a bolas from his bag. The future-Kirby had rattled off instructions on how to use it, but Toby hadn't really been listening. He chided himself for not being professional and hoped he could improvise.

Toby swung the bolas over his head; the momentum charged the superpower stored inside each tethered weight. As Pete was about to incinerate Worm, Toby released the weapon—

It was a perfect shot. The bolas wrapped around Pete's arms, pinning them against his body as he fired. His super-blast tore into his own leg and he howled in agony as his flesh was burnt away to the bone. It was a horrific sight to witness, and it was fortunately blocked when the bolas released its power and trapped Pete inside an opaque body-hugging bubble that silenced his screams.

Worm didn't wait around. He ran across the clearing and almost made it to the trees—until Toby's energy-whip snaked around his throat and pulled him to the ground so hard that the villain's head cracked on a rock, knocking him out cold.

Toby looked around at the three prone figures. His mind was racing at how Pete's selfishness had caused the situation to deteriorate so rapidly. Finally healed, he walked across to Kirby. The man had a jagged cut across his temple, but Toby could still feel a pulse.

Toby felt like crying, both from the relief that nobody had been killed and the shock that his own friend had been willing to sacrifice him to Worm's men.

He managed to leap up the pyramid in three stages, dragging Worm's prone body behind him. He couldn't risk the villain getting loose as he had no way to stop him if he did. He placed Worm in the cryogenic chamber and sealed him in the deep sleep from which he would not wake until Toby's father found him in the future.

Toby shook his head. No wonder that the future Kirby had no recollection of what had happened today. It wasn't him who imprisoned Worm after all, and Toby had only done it out of necessity.

His plan to leap down from the pyramid was thwarted when he discovered that his downloaded powers had run out. Toby hoped that he wouldn't face any other threats.

He carefully climbed down the ancient structure. On reaching the bottom he was alarmed to discover that Pete was missing. He couldn't find any trace of where the traitor had gone. Toby tried to push the thought from his mind and instead focused on helping Kirby.


It had taken Toby a day to get back to the airbase, dragging Kirby on a stretcher he had made from broken branches tied together with vines. He had found enough water to drink, but he was now starving and shaking from fatigue.

# Déjà vu

Army medics took Kirby away and tended to Toby's needs.

'You don't look bad for a kid who's been lost in the jungle,' commented the medic as he dabbed Toby's forehead.

'I need food.' Toby closed his eyes as he felt a sudden wave of dizziness.

*'You don't look bad for a kid who's been lost in the jungle,' repeated the medic as he dabbed Toby's forehead.* Toby's eyes flicked open and the medic looked at him in surprise. 'What'd I say?'

'I've just had déjà vu,' said Toby urgently.

The medic looked puzzled. Then the world flexed once more and Toby was hurtled through time.

# The Jigsaw Completed

The flickering neon light compounded Toby's headache. He shielded his eyes and looked around the room. It was a bare medical room without a single other patient. He sat up and swung his legs out of the bed. He tried to recall the last few . . . hours? Days? He had no idea.

He recalled Kirby talking to him, but his voice was distorted and distant. Toby had woken a few times to see the same unsmiling nurse who had stood over him after Pete had broken out of the hospital. This was certainly his week for head injuries and he wondered how much permanent damage he might have sustained.

Then it occurred to him that he was back at the Hero Foundation. The room was modern, the clothes he wore were exact replicas of what he had been wearing for the last few days but they were new.

The door opened and Kirby strode in looking more

frustrated than ever. He didn't offer any greeting when he saw that Toby was awake.

'Suriname and Qinghai Province in China. They're gone.'

'Gone where?' said Toby, trying to stop his head from spinning.

'Time has ceased to exist there. Lord Eon has taken them, stolen the time from millions of people.'

'Why those locations? It doesn't make any sense. Neither of those places are together . . . are they?' Toby was good at geography, but not *that* good.

Kirby called up a map on a large display screen like the one in his office.

'They're *almost* on opposite sides of the world.'

'But why?'

'*Why, why, why?* Is that all you ever say?' snapped Kirby. Toby felt his cheeks burn. What kind of attitude was that to show somebody who saved your life, no matter how many years ago it had been?

'Sorry I asked,' he muttered. 'Not that you bother telling me anything in the first place.'

Kirby took a deep breath and calmed down. 'Lord Eon does not see the world like we do. There are no countries, no mountains, no weather, nothing like that. He sees the world in an abstract form. He can only see in time and space, atoms and quantum forces. The other places he seized around the globe were nothing more than random probes into our world. He was feeding and testing for weak points in time. Now he has found two virtually *opposite*.'

'How can he use that?'

'Think, boy!' snapped Kirby, once again losing his patience. 'Think of the north and south poles. What do they do?'

Toby crossed to the plasma screen and stared at the map. He noticed the corner of the screen was chipped in the same place as the one in Kirby's office. In fact, it *was* the same screen. Was money so tight they had to recycle furniture?

'They're cold,' said Toby, recalling the time he'd spent fighting Doc Tempest in Antarctica. When this didn't get a flicker of a smile from Kirby he got more serious. 'And they form the magnetic poles.'

Kirby clicked his fingers. 'Exactly. In this case Eon is forming chrono-poles. Think of them as diverting time and space as we know it around the planet. The stronger he gets, the more powerful this time stream becomes—and we all get sucked into it. Like being pulled into a black hole except we won't die. And we will all be unable to escape. Already our sensors are picking up a growing number of Time-Storms appearing along this new "pole".'

Toby was only half-listening. He was looking at the signet ring on Kirby's right hand. The *opposite* hand to the one he had worn it on in the jungle. Kirby clicked his fingers again. 'Pay attention!'

Toby forced his gaze back to Kirby. He had a growing sense that something wasn't right, but he couldn't think what it was.

'How did I get here?'

Kirby frowned at Toby. 'Don't you remember?'

Toby shook his head. 'Look, I know the situation with Eon is critical, but I'm feeling a little freaked out right now and need you to backtrack to how I came here.'

'You remember Japan?'

'I remember fighting that girl, Jen, and Pete for the piece of the Temporal Dilator.'

'Yes, the crucial piece that you *lost* to the enemy,' said Kirby harshly.

Toby ignored him. 'Then Lord Eon appeared and . . .'

'And sent you and Pete back in time. This we know.'

'Do you know what happened next?'

Kirby avoiding making eye contact. 'You didn't say.'

*You really don't remember*, thought Toby. 'You were there.' Kirby's gaze remained unblinking. 'It was during the war, when you were looking for Worm.'

'Ah yes. Well, as you know, I have no memory of that event. After I incarcerated Worm . . . I remember nothing else.'

# The Jigsaw Completed

Toby frowned, wanting to test how much Kirby really did remember, but another question was more pressing. 'Why did he send us there?'

Kirby looked thoughtful. 'Eon would have sent you back in time for a reason. What happened?'

Toby didn't think now was the right time to correct Kirby's own history.

'We put Worm in cryogenic storage,' he said carefully. 'He wanted me there to do that . . . my God! I know why he needed us there! You said it yourself, events in the present affect the past! If I hadn't run into Eon in Japan he would not have sent Pete and me back to the nineteen forties. We wouldn't have stopped Worm and put him in deep freeze. If he hadn't been in deep freeze then my dad wouldn't have woken him and he would never have met Basilisk.'

Kirby's eyes were wide as he picked up Toby's train of thought. 'So Basilisk wouldn't have been able to break into Diablo Island to spring Viral. An act that caused the subsequent prison riots and facilitated Eon's eventual escape.'

'And by taking Emily, Lord Eon provoked Pete enough to make sure we *would* end up fighting against one another . . . '

Toby was blown away by the implication. Eon himself had said he needed the boys. 'He needed me alive *now* to make sure the past happened. He was *retro-planning* his escape! He planned for us to go back!'

'The present affects the past,' muttered Kirby. 'Incredible. He didn't have to change time because it had already happened.'

'You can't change the past, only the future,' intoned Toby.

Kirby snapped out of his daydream. 'So it is thanks to you that Lord Eon escaped. Congratulations.'

Once again Toby felt his face flush. He recalled something that Kirby had said weeks ago when they were at the old Foundation Headquarters before they'd been destroyed. Kirby had made a passing comment that Toby didn't yet know what it was like to have a friend betray him. He must have been referring to the fight Toby would have with Pete in Mexico. Which meant he knew more than he was letting on.

'You already knew what would happen, didn't you? You almost said it back at the original Foundation HQ. Why didn't you tell me? Why didn't you warn me about Pete?'

Kirby brushed his hand as if to discard the idea. 'Nonsense! You're imagining things. Now, focus on matters to hand. That Jen girl got the last piece of the Temporal Dilator, so they have two.'

'Then why don't we ask to work together against a common enemy?'

# The Jigsaw Completed

'Not a chance. Our spies have reported that they have already replicated what they think the piece Eon destroyed looks like.'

'Can they do that?'

'Maybe. We've tried but had no success, but it appears they have tracked down fragments of the original meteor. Your friend Jen is picking up the replicated Dilator pieces from a lab in Chicago and assembling them there. So you will steal the items en route. Lord Eon is already casting his net wide, so you will have to take what we have. Once you steal their components then assemble the Temporal Dilator and activate it. The fate of the world hangs in the balance on this. If you have to kill the girl, then gather some courage and do it. Now eat and get your strength up.' He pointed to a plastic tray, its compartments filled with unappetizing, congealed, unidentifiable *stuff*. 'I will prepare your departure.'

Kirby strode from the room leaving Toby alone once again.

Something wasn't right. He knew Primes were cowards, so why weren't they gathering an army of Downloaders to do the mission like the villains were? And where was Lorna in all this? What was she doing that was so vitally important? Why was he being kept isolated and his powers limited?

After the pain he had been through with Pete, Toby

had had enough. He wanted answers. He crossed to the door. It was sealed like the one in Kirby's office. And, in the same way, the lock was useless. He had no trouble sliding the door open.

Toby stepped into an empty corridor. There was no sign of Kirby. He was at a dead end with another heavy door at the far end. This one wouldn't open no matter how hard he tried. He was trapped.

Toby punched the wall in frustration—and his hand passed right through! For a second he thought that he had super-strength, but then remembered that his powers had abandoned him in Mexico. He examined the wall: it was thin plasterboard. Weird.

With growing anxiety, Toby pulled chunks of the wall apart until he created a space big enough to climb through. He stepped into the darkness beyond.

Judging by the cool breeze and the echoing acoustics he was standing in a large space. It took his eyes several seconds to adjust—and then he gasped.

He was standing in a large empty warehouse. Behind him, wooden trellises supported plasterboard walls. He walked around the structure, realizing that Kirby's office, the equipment centre, and the medical ward were all . . . fake sets. It was as if he was in a movie studio.

'This is seriously weird,' he muttered to himself.

Across the hangar he could see light seeping through

# The Jigsaw Completed

the edges of a door. He crossed the cavernous floor space and listened. He heard muffled talking beyond. He glanced around for anything he could use as a weapon. Stacks of wood and spare set dressings were propped against the wall. There was a tool chest brimming with potential weapons. He took a heavy wrench and gingerly opened the door.

The corridor was brightly lit and two burly guards were standing there dressed in black uniforms. They did a double take when they saw Toby step from the doorway wielding the wrench. He knocked one out and dived aside as the second guard scrabbled for his gun.

In blind panic, Toby threw the wrench at the man, clobbering him squarely between the eyes. He fell, unconscious. With great effort, Toby dragged both bodies into the studio. He didn't want to take their bulky rifles but he found a stun gun in the utility belt of one. That would do.

Toby closed the door behind him and tiptoed down the corridor. He reached another sliding doorway that opened as he approached.

He found himself outside, on a curved walkway that led to another building made of white towers and domes. It looked futuristic. Toby crossed the walkway. Peering over the balustrade, he saw waves crashing below and realized that the walkway connected two islands. To his right was a large island that stood from

the sea on a sheer spar of rock. The network of buildings there looked like a mini-city. He saw other walkways leading from yet more islands circling the central
mini-city. It was an impressive complex.

Toby ran across to the smaller island. Another door
opened automatically as he approached and he entered
a warm, air-conditioned corridor that branched in two
separate directions. He had no idea which one to take.

Then he heard a familiar voice. Eric Kirby was speaking from a nearby room. He edged to the door, worried
that it might automatically open if he got too near and
alert Kirby to his presence.

'The boy has failed twice!' said the voice Toby
remembered hearing last time he eavesdropped on
Kirby's conversation.

'But he is good,' insisted Kirby. This time Toby didn't
feel happy about the adulation. 'He can do this. Who
else are we going to send? We can't trust anybody!'

'You should go yourself?'

'Me? As soon as they recognized me the Temporal
Dilator would be placed beyond our reach.'

Toby was desperate to see who was talking and
wished he had superpowers to get inside unseen. Life
was much too difficult when you had to rely on your
wits.

Toby noticed a mesh grille high on the wall. It must
have once been a narrow window to light the room. It

wasn't big enough to climb through, but he might be able to peer inside. Toby jumped, his fingers digging into the lip of the sill. He grunted as he lifted his chin level to the mesh. His muscles burned from the effort, reminding him how unfit he had become depending on his superpowers.

The room beyond was relatively bare, with only a table, a computer, and a few chairs. Kirby was sitting at the table, looking anxious. Toby could see the back of a huge man who looked as if he had no neck.

'And I can't go either!' said the neckless man.

'So we're stuck with the boy.'

'We can always send more Downloaders.'

'Like you did in Germany? Look where that got us! They're selfish and undisciplined. Toby has values and morals and we can use them to play him to our advantage.'

Toby's arms started to shake from the effort of keeping himself up. Kirby stood, scratching his face.

'I suppose it's only for one last mission.'

'Exactly. Then you will be the saviour of the day. It will be all hail, "Momentum",' said Kirby sarcastically. Toby had heard that name before but he couldn't think where. 'And I want my rightful position in the new Council as we agreed.'

Toby nearly fell at the words. 'The Council' could only mean one thing—and it reminded him how he knew the name 'Momentum'; he was a member of the Council of Evil! Why had Kirby betrayed them all?

'After what's been going on around here, there won't be much of a Council left if you don't hurry!'

'This damn disguise is giving me cramp!' complained Kirby as he stood. He shook his head—and Toby saw his skin sag as if it was made from rubber. His face stretched and deformed until it snapped back into the unfamiliar face of a grey-haired middle-aged man. 'That's so much better!' said the fake-Kirby.

Toby fell from the mesh and landed hard and loud on the floor. His head was reeling—Kirby was a shape-changing villain . . . that meant Toby had been working for the Council of Evil all this time!

The past few days rocketed through his memory like a bullet train. Jen had said he was the enemy . . . but she never used the words hero or villain. He had just *assumed* he knew which side he was fighting for. It explained why he had been confined to a fake set and his powers limited. Of course, they wouldn't want him to download any attack powers in case he worked things out and turned on them. That was why he couldn't access the real Hero.com from the computer in Japan—he had been barred!

Which could only mean the Hero Foundation thought he had switched sides along with Pete!

They thought he was a rogue hero.

# The Jigsaw Completed

Jen had hinted as much when she said people were looking for him and her bosses wanted to speak to him. Now that he knew, he felt that the truth had been obvious from the very moment he opened his eyes after Pete's escape.

The door swished open and the shapeshifter ran out. 'I thought I heard—'

He froze when he saw Toby, his face and body snapping back into the shape of Kirby. But it was too late, Toby knew.

'Kirby' lunged for him, but Toby stabbed the stun gun into the man's stomach and pulled the trigger. The shapeshifter howled and his face rapidly flickered through dozens of disguises before he fell on the floor, paralysed, his face stuck in an ugly combination of his last three guises.

Toby sprinted down the corridor as Momentum waddled from the room. He saw that the shapeshifter was down, and glimpsed the back of Toby rounding a corner.

Toby reached a crossroads; two of the junctions had sturdy looking steel doors. He ran towards one and it opened on his approach. He ducked through, spinning round as the door closed. He rammed the stun gun into the lock and short-circuited the mechanism. His plan worked and the door jammed.

Momentum pounded it from the other side. 'Open up!'

Toby smiled at his own ingenuity. A siren suddenly wailed across the complex, an automated male voice repeating the words:

'Alert! Prisoner escape!'

Toby turned round—and froze.

The room was a large canteen, and it was filled with several dozen Council of Evil guards and assorted supervillains in an eclectic mix of costumes. They were all staring at him, some with forks midway to their mouths.

'Oh boy,' muttered Toby.

Then everybody seemed to move at once. Guards went for their weapons and the Primes threw down their lunch trays. There was *no* escape for Toby.

Momentum broke through the door. True to his name he had taken a long run up, gaining momentum with every footstep. By the time he hit the solid steel blast doors he possessed the destructive force of a missile.

He smashed through several tables, scattering the hired help like matchsticks before he skidded to a halt. Toby saw he was snorting like a bull. He raised an accusing finger at Toby.

'I want him alive!'

The room moved en masse in pursuit of Toby.

Toby sprinted for all he was worth down the corridor, dodging around stacked tables and computers on trolleys. It was like fleeing in a high-tech school. His

# The Jigsaw Completed

shaky legs were forgotten as survival instinct kicked in. Behind him the corridor was a mass of jostling guards and villains. The front line unleashed their barrage of weaponry in one massive volley—

Lightning bolts, jagged icicles, fireballs, sticky webbing, lasers, and glue blobs smashed into the walls, floor, and ceiling. Sparks blasted computer equipment and fireballs caused everything else to explode.

Toby skidded round a corner as the ceiling collapsed behind him. He could say one thing about the Council of Evil—*they were really bad shots!*

He knew the rubble wouldn't hold them for long. Already he could hear a plethora of superpowers being used to shatter the barricade. He turned another corner and ran into two guards who were sprinting in his direction. They automatically raised their weapons.

'They've got the prisoner back there! We need backup!'

The guards nodded and ran towards the noise. Toby's gamble that they wouldn't know what the prisoner looked like had paid off.

He ran down another corridor; this one offered windows with panoramic views across the sea and the violent waves crashing below. There was no escape that way without powers. He reached a door midway down and took the risk of turning in there.

It was an office, and it was a mess. One wall was

covered with a map of the world that was thick with pins. A sign said they showed Downloader density on Villain.net.

Boxes were stacked against one wall. They were full of super-shades, the sunglasses he'd used in Cambodia. Toby shoved several pairs into his pocket, in case they would prove useful later.

But other than the door through which he had come in, there was no way out. He caught the sounds of an explosion deeper in the complex and guessed that his pursuers had finally cleared a path through the fallen ceiling.

He looked around desperately—then back to the Villain.net usage chart. He couldn't use Hero.com . . . but could he use Villain.net?

With shaking hands he accessed the desktop computer. Like Hero.com, the Villain.net URL wasn't a simple case of typing in the address. You had to be invited to join either super-platform.

Or be able to access the Intranet.

The screen logged him straight onto the COE Intranet: the internal network that wasn't accessible to the outside world. A few clicks of the mouse, and he found what he was looking for—the Villain.net screen. This was the first time he had ever seen it, and straight away he could see how the villains had pirated the design and technology from the Hero Foundation.

# The Jigsaw Completed

He scrolled through the stick-figure icons. Like its hero counterpart, the villain site didn't label what the powers were. He could be downloading anything. He clicked on several familiar looking options. The screen flickered as the system transferred the powers. The Council had even stolen the new method of transferring them.

Toby heard the angry mob approaching. It would be a grossly unfair fight—one he had little chance of winning. He glanced back at the Villain.net site and spotted an icon similar to one he and Pete had discussed months previously, back in the days when they would explore the list and guess what powers the icons represented. He hoped that Pete had been right about this one.

Before he clicked he took one last look around the office and tore a map from the wall. He stuffed it in his jacket just as the mob ran past the door. Most didn't even look into the room, but a villain with a one-piece bodysuit, covered in porcupine-like spikes, stopped and stared at him in surprise.

'He's here!' yelled Spiky.

Without looking, Toby clicked on the icon and then raised his hands. He felt the power transfer, and somehow knew how to control it. He activated the unusual superpower.

He winked at Spiky then allowed himself to be

sucked into the computer screen as his entire body was digitized in a second.

He was now in cyberspace and heading away from the Council of Evil at the speed of light.

# Nicking Time

Cyberspace was a twisting world of interconnected tunnels of light. The walls were so transparent Toby could 'see' beyond them, to the complex network of tunnels and supernova flashes of processed information. Bright lights of every colour and shape zoomed past him in the tunnel: they were pieces of data being bounced around the system. Some fragments were tiny glowing envelopes representing emails, others were fiercely glowing red balls of fury that were heavily encrypted files.

Toby was now a mass of electrical impulses, yet he could still sense the world around him as he bounced through the network faster than he had ever moved before.

A massive cluster of lights the size of a city lay ahead, revolving in a tightly packed sphere that resembled a swirling galaxy. It was one of many servers that Toby found himself being bounced from. Once inside he was surrounded by digital representations of everything—from banks whose pillars and bricks were made from glowing binary numbers to shops of every description. Personal social network pages flashed like billboards with glowing red portals preventing the casual viewer from accessing personal information. Toby swerved out of the way of a giant hand that reached out for him—it was a digital avatar, a personal representative of the user in the real world.

The experience was exhilarating, but Toby knew he had more pressing business to hand. He had to focus on his destination. He needed to get to Chicago, and as close to Jen as possible.

He locked on to a Chicago server and felt a magnetic pull as his body was drawn down yet more tunnels and through dazzling nexuses. A faint pulse on the horizon indicated that his destination was close. He hit a server and a virtual representation of Chicago appeared around him, constructed from millions of tiny moving lights. He recognized the iconic Sears Tower—now all he had to do was find Jen. He thought about locating her CUCI. Hero.com used the regular byways of the Internet to transfer its powers, and likewise the CUCI information pulsed out across the net as well as on its own dedicated wireless frequency.

He found her signal, shining like a beacon, and rushed towards it—but bounced off a flaming wall that sprang up before him. It was surprisingly painful. The firewall blocked his access. He would have to find another exit—and fast.

Hayden Daniels was eleven, and he was a serious game-head. He had already won several State games championships, and when his parents saw the cash prizes he was capable of winning they actively encouraged him to stay inside and play games. Except for the arduous trips to school, Hayden hadn't been out of the house for almost a year and his chair was beginning to get too small for his expanding bottom.

He was on the final level of his new console game *Soul Destroyer*. Once he had beaten the end of level baddie he would have mastered the game, ready for his first World Championship and the $100,000 prize.

He was so immersed in the game that when the TV screen flickered and Toby was thrown into the room, landing amongst scattered crisp packets, Hayden didn't even blink.

Toby climbed to his feet, wiping crumbs and a sliver of cold pizza from his jacket. He nodded casually at Hayden.

'How you doing?' Then he ran from the room.

Hayden stared at the controller in his hand—then back at the screen.

'Awesome!' he declared.

Toby sprinted out of the apartment block. It was getting dark outside and streetlights were slowly turning on, but there was still enough light to see down the street. He had chosen an exit ahead of Jen's route. While he was immersed in cyberspace he was able to access an online map and the local information was instantly absorbed into his brain. He made a note to download this power next time he had to cram for an exam.

Jen had turned off Highway 55 and was heading north on South State Street. A convoy of three military style armoured cars rolled past him and his internal beacon flashed showing Jen's CUCI. She was in the lead vehicle.

Six police motorcycle outriders flanked the convoy; three police cars went ahead, sirens wailing to clear a path. The armoured cars were followed by four black SWAT vans, no doubt brimming with heavily armed, but superpowerless, Enforcers. The Foundation were clearly expecting him, and they weren't taking any chances. If he flew over he would be shot out of the sky. He would have to hope the rest of his pirated powers would work.

Toby ran towards the lead truck and then quantum

tunnelled into the cab. It was a quieter and more accurate mode of travel than teleportation.

He appeared on the seat next to Jen. She turned and screamed at him. The driver next to her, weighed down by body armour, looked at him with wild eyes.

'Wait!' yelled Toby.

Jen was fast—her hand was already clamped across his throat, pinning him to the window. Toby felt her high-voltage touch burn through every nerve of his skin and his body jerked, numbing his extremities. Smoke poured from his skin. The pain was excruciating.

'Stop,' he wheezed.

Jen stopped the current, but kept a hand across his throat. Immediately Toby's body started to heal.

'Keep moving,' she ordered the driver. 'This could be an ambush.'

'It is,' croaked Toby. It was difficult to talk with the pressure on his throat. 'But I'm on your side.'

Jen laughed. 'Yeah, right!'

'I've been set up! I swear!' Jen frowned and loosened her grip, but she made it clear if Toby tried to move she wouldn't be so lenient. 'I thought I was working for Kirby. But he was a shapeshifter working for Momentum.'

'The Council member?'

'Yeah. They made me think I was working for the

Foundation, they had a set and everything. I thought you were the villain.'

'Me?'

'Why do you think I saved you? I'm not a bad guy!'

'I suspected that you hadn't fully crossed the line. That there was still some old Toby inside that could show mercy. But after you sank that cruise liner . . .'

'That was Pete! And the person I thought was Kirby said he'd despatched a Hero crew to rescue people.'

'Nobody helped, Toby. It was a terrible disaster and everybody blamed you for it.'

'I was teleported away before I could do anything. Don't forget, Pete got that piece of the Temporal Dilator from *me*. He gave it to Lord Eon! Why do you think every time you were in danger I tried to do the right thing? I could have left you alone with Pete in the Bullet Train, but I didn't.'

Jen hesitated. '*That's* why you were fighting Pete . . . I thought it was odd once he crossed to your . . . to the villain's side.'

'I assumed *you two* were working together, and I thought it was weird you were fighting each other. You must believe me! I've been used. It wasn't until Eon threw me back in time and I met the real Kirby that I realized the contemporary Kirby was acting completely differently from normal. But I don't understand how it all happened.'

# Nicking Time

Jen released him, but didn't lower her guard. 'When Pete escaped from the hospital we found you had gone too. Eric Kirby was left unconscious on the floor. We assumed that you had both attacked him and fled.'

'Why would I do that?'

Jen shrugged. 'That was the mystery, but we figured it was connected to your sister's relationship with Jake Hunter.' She saw the puzzled look cross Toby's face. 'You do know about Jake, don't you?'

'He was dating my sister. I do know that.'

Jen shook her head in amazement. 'Toby, Jake is an agent for Villain.net!' Toby was thunderstruck. He couldn't think of anything to say. Jen continued. 'We don't know whether your sister knew that, but when she vanished, well, we didn't know what to think. Love can make people do weird things. And if your sister has switched sides, and we knew Pete already had, then it was a small step to believe that you had.'

But Toby was still thinking about Jake. 'I didn't know . . . Jake a *villain*?'

'They call him Dark Hunter.'

Toby rubbed his temples. It was all so obvious.

'Did he know we were heroes?'

'When he visited Pete at the hospital, after the destruction of Hero HQ, he did. He needs Pete to help him with a problem. We don't know what it is. In some ways Hunter did us all a favour by convincing Pete *not* to work with Lord Eon. Maybe there's a hero some-where inside him,' she said with a thin smile.

'Where is Lorna? Kirby told me . . . the shapeshifter told me that she was on a special mission for the Foundation.'

'I'm afraid not. We don't know where she is. We do know that she was last seen with Hunter.'

Toby felt anger course through his veins. 'I swear I'll bring down the Council for this!'

'I think Hunter's doing a fine job on his own. He was appointed to the Council of Evil some weeks ago. Shall we just say, the boy doesn't disappoint. Anyway, assum-ing I buy your story about being misled, why are you here? You should hand yourself in to the Foundation. There are a lot of upset people looking for you, which has been difficult since your CUCI was removed.' Toby looked at the scar on his wrist—so that's where it came from. Momentum and the shapeshifter must have taken it out and replaced it with a Villain.net one 'They think you're a traitor.'

Toby had a million questions buzzing around his head but Lord Eon was the immediate problem—if he wasn't brought down then neither side could win.

'I overheard Momentum say that you were develop-ing replica Dilator pieces in a lab to re-create the miss-ing ones but on the train you said the pieces couldn't be replicated. To be honest I've lost count who has what. They told me the Dilator part I saved in Germany was stolen, but I suppose that's a lie?'

'We still have the part you saved in Germany. You . . . sorry, the Council . . . got the Cambodia piece and I got the one in Japan. Which leaves the one Eon destroyed, which we think we may have copied. And of course I would tell you they were impossible to copy, I thought you were my enemy! I'm amazed I survived Eon's rampage. The whole of Tokyo has been removed from the grid. That's nearly thirteen million people he is leeching from.'

'So the Council only has one part of the Temporal Dilator?'

'That's the one we need. We haven't been able to replicate it.'

'Then I have some good news. It's on its way here.' Jen didn't understand. 'That's why I came. The Council are planning an ambush.'

'Where?'

The convoy reached the intersection at East 18th Street where the city's midway rail line joined the famous elevated older green line. The convoy was making a left turn as the elevated train tracks above them collapsed with a crunch of concrete and steel.

Jen and Toby were thrown forward in the cab as the driver slammed on the brakes. A massive wall of dust washed over the vehicles, killing visibility.

Toby jumped from the cab and looked around, his eyes stinging from the dust. He couldn't see a thing. He groped into his pockets and pulled out a pair of super-shades. The world around him was bathed in thermal colours.

He could see Enforcers leap from the SWAT vans, but they were unable to see any targets. Toby saw Jen flailing next to him. He grabbed her arm and forced a second pair of super-shades on her.

'Get the Dilator together! I'll hold them off.'

She ran to the back of the truck. Toby walked through the dust. There was no sign of the attackers.

Toby walked in a wide circle—still he couldn't see anybody. Then he heard Jen scream for help.

He ran back towards the trucks. A light breeze was starting to scatter the dust. He could see Jen with her back to a truck, a bulging pack over her shoulder. In front of her, climbing from the last security truck, was Pete. He was standing a good two feet taller and held two pieces of the Temporal Dilator in a case—one he had stolen from the back of the truck, and the one Toby had saved in Cambodia.

Behind him stood ten COE guards, all pointing weapons at Jen.

'I don't really want to kill you,' snarled Pete. 'So just give me the damn bag.' He held up the pieces he already had. 'And then we can deal with Eon.'

# Nicking Time

'You're all monsters!'

'I'm no monster. I'm what everybody made me.'

'You did this to yourself, Pete,' said Toby stepping forwards.

Pete was startled to see him. 'Tobe! You survived!'

'No thanks to you.'

'I thought I'd . . . you were dead,' said Pete.

Did Toby hear a trace of emotion in his voice? Pete's expression remained a snarl. 'You're surrounded and powerless, Tobe. So shut up and give me the Dilator pieces. Don't make this any harder than—'

Toby was growing bored with the monologue. He sensed movement in the dust next to him—the reassuring shape of armed Enforcers. Toby didn't let Pete finish his demand—he fired at his friend.

Slimy glue-like balls spat from his mouth and stuck Pete to the ground, spreading around his body. Because there was no energy to absorb, Pete didn't increase in bulk, but he was firmly rooted to the spot. It was worth the bad taste in Toby's mouth; although he had originally raised his hand thinking the glue would shoot from there.

The Enforcers opened fire at exactly the same time as the COE guards. Toby lunged for Jen, dragging her for cover under the armoured truck.

It was complete mayhem as Enforcers and COE goons scattered for cover.

HERO.CÖM

'We've got to help the Enforcers!' shouted Jen.

Toby looked out. His thermal vision revealed that Pete had torn away the glue bonds and was pushing a COE trooper towards an empty SWAT van. They both climbed inside, the trooper behind the wheel. Obviously Pete had thought having two pieces was victory enough, and, unable to fly or teleport while he had the pieces, had found another means of escape.

'He's getting away!' said Toby as he pulled Jen from under the truck. They ran in pursuit, but the van was much too fast. 'Let's fly!' Toby lifted into the air.

'I can't! I've got two parts here,' said Jen indicating her pack. 'Besides, I don't like flying. I can't do it.'

Toby hesitated. He needed to stop Pete from his rendezvous with the COE but he couldn't risk leaving Jen and the Temporal Dilator pieces behind in the middle of a battle.

'What *can* you do?' he asked desperately.

Jen lifted her super-shades onto her forehead and smiled, pointing to a police bike lying on its side. 'I can ride one of those!'

The powerful Kawasaki motorbike was the first real motorbike Toby had ever ridden, and it was almost as exhilarating as flying. He clung to Jen as she skilfully weaved the bike through traffic, towards the SWAT van.

They were heading downtown. After a few hair-raising turns they shot over one of the many bridges straddling the Chicago River. The gap between vehicles had narrowed—which was Pete's cue to make an appearance.

He booted the SWAT van doors off their hinges, forcing Jen to skid around them. One door slammed into the windscreen of a car next to them. Pete followed it with a powerful cobalt blast that tore up the road, narrowly missing the bike as Jen deftly veered aside.

Toby returned fire—a series of energy hoops shot from his fingers, growing like smoke rings until they hit the side of the van, sending it onto two wheels. The driver fought to keep control, bringing it back onto four wheels as Toby spat out yet more glue-balls. One accidentally plastered across the windscreen of an oncoming car—another stuck Pete's hand to the inside roof of the van just as he fired again. His blast tore a hole through the vehicle roof.

'Nice one!' shouted Jen.

Pete fired with his free arm, blowing up a delivery truck right in front of them. The force of the explosion threw both Jen and Toby to the ground. The bike skidded on its side in a shower of sparks. If it hadn't been for their regeneration powers they would have been road kill.

Toby helped Jen stand. 'Are you OK?'

'Just about. Where did he go?'

They looked wildly around—the SWAT van had taken a side street. Toby slid his shades back on and switched to X-ray vision. Jen immediately became a skeleton as she moved to the bike, which looked like a mass of black and semi-transparent parts.

Toby squinted harder, willing the super-shades to increase their range. They made the traffic that was halting around him become completely transparent. The walls of the skyscraper in front of him peeled away until he could see the street on the far side—and the tail end of the SWAT van skidding around a corner.

'I see him!' he yelled.

Jen pulled alongside and Toby climbed aboard the motorbike, which was a weird experience, as he could no longer see it—in fact when he looked down he could see through the road surface to the sewers beyond.

'Which way?' shouted Jen as she accelerated so fast that the heavy Kawasaki popped a wheelie. She followed Toby's pointing finger.

'Back across the river.'

The traffic melted away from Toby's vision as it got nearer. He targeted the SWAT van.

'Left! Left!' he screamed.

Jen looked at the massive tower to their left—there was no way through it. 'How?'

Toby sighed as the truck turned another bend—it looked as if Pete's driver was lost. 'Jen, are you blind?'

'Well, I can see the massive skyscraper in our way!'

She turned down the next road, but the SWAT van was in the road parallel, visible only to Toby.

'Which way?'

'There!' said Toby pointing at a passing row of shops. 'We're gaining! Go right! Right!'

Frustrated he pulled the super-shades from Jen's forehead down over her eyes and toggled the switch. Immediately the buildings melted away and she could see that the truck was close.

'There!' shouted Toby. 'See it now?'

Jen nodded. It looked as though the side street ahead would bring them behind the van. 'Hold on!' she yelled and leaned to the right.

A multitude of screams filled Toby's ears as they took the side road, but he could see nothing. The motorbike suddenly ploughed through a window; the impact almost dragged them off the vehicle.

Toby lifted his super-shades up to see what was going on. He couldn't believe it—

'Jen! What are you doing?'

She pulled her super-shades up and was horrified to

discover they had driven into an indoor shopping centre. What she had presumed was a side street was in fact the wide mall hall. She could only yell as they approached the top of a set of escalators—

Shoppers watched in awe as the motorcycle ramped off the top level of the mezzanine—over a dining area—and through a huge window on the far side.

The bike landed on top of a taxicab, crushing the roof. Jen wrestled for control, but it was a miracle they didn't fall off as they dropped from the taxi to the road. The SWAT van was now straight ahead.

Pete had watched their amazing exit and ducked as Toby spat several more glue blobs at him. They missed their target as the van bumped other vehicles aside.

The vehicles zigzagged through the streets—Toby caught a street sign: East Monroe Street.

They passed the huge lattice structure of the Jay Pritzker Pavilion on their left—then followed the SWAT van as it jumped a red light and smashed its way through an intersection.

Jen skilfully shot through a gap between two trucks. The street became open and park-like. Ahead they could see countless boat masts in the Marina. Beyond, the twilight sky was a mass of overactive clouds. Lightning crackled in the heavens. Toby felt a sense of dread—Lord Eon was approaching.

# Nicking Time

'Aim for the wheels!' yelled Jen.

She arced the motorbike wide into the *oncoming* traffic. Cars honked their horns as she weaved between them. It was dangerous but it gave Toby the angle he needed. He spat globules at the van's wheels—

He scored a perfect hit. The two side wheels immediately locked as the sticky substance swelled over the tyres. The driver wrestled the controls but the van slewed sideways and toppled over, scraping across the road in a shower of sparks.

Pete was jettisoned from the vehicle. He rolled hard, knocking aside a pair of cars as he gained mass. He flipped acrobatically onto his feet and ran into the Marina.

'Follow him!' Toby yelled.

Pete was limping; his regeneration powers appeared to be slow in activating. Perhaps his powers were starting to wear off?

Toby and Jen easily caught him as he ran across a wooden boardwalk that stretched between expensive yachts. He cradled the two Temporal Dilator pieces to his chest.

Toby flew off the bike and glued Pete's feet to the wooden deck as he orbited him. Pete stopped for a moment, but with a grunt of effort he lifted his foot, pulling the board with it.

Toby struck him with a power ring, and Pete sprawled across the ground, growing bigger.

Pete laughed. 'Whatever you do to me, you're only making me more powerful! You can't beat me!'

Toby pointed at the Time-Storm that was approaching from the south-east. 'We'll both lose if Eon gets here! Give me the pieces!'

'Come and get them,' taunted Pete.

'I don't have time for this! Be reasonable.'

'There you go again, telling me what to do! Not this time! If anyone is going to save the day, it'll be me. On my terms!'

'One last chance, Pete.'

Pete hurled a bolt at Toby slamming him off the boardwalk and onto the deck of a yacht. Toby howled in pain.

'Or what?' snarled Pete.

Jen stepped forward, hand poised. 'Unlike Toby, I'm not your friend. I don't have any qualms about frying you.'

'You won't shoot me because you won't risk damaging the artefacts.'

Jen hesitated. Pete smiled.

'You see, I have control now.'

Then a yellow jolt suddenly coursed through Pete's body, paralysing him and freezing the surprised expression on his face.

# Nicking Time

'Sorry, mate, but you really have to learn to stop the cocky victory speeches.' Toby pulled the two weighty artefacts from Pete's hands.

'What did you do to him?'

'It's a cool paralysing power I downloaded.'

'From where?' Jen asked suspiciously.

'From Villain.net,' said Toby sheepishly. 'Help me put this thing together.'

He ignored Jen's questioning glance and examined the two parts he had. They were squid-like, with long branching tendrils. He knew one was the replica made by the Foundation.

'They both look real.'

'The Foundation found part of the meteor that was originally used. The material is the same, we better hope the shape is right.'

'It looks like I remember.'

Jen extracted the remaining two artefacts from her backpack. One was the black pencil-case-sized box that Toby and Lorna had recovered in Germany. Inside was a large diamond with a fine mesh of meteor iron wrought around it.

'This was what was in the security truck in Germany,' she explained. 'It was how Eon was originally caught and stored in Diablo Island. That's why the Foundation had it in the first place.' She held up the final section. It was a T-shaped, thin pin. 'And that is what I got in Japan. We have to figure out how all this goes together.'

They both looked around as the wind increased in force. They watched in horror as the Time-Storm rolled across the city. They were so close they could see that the clouds reached to the ground. People were fleeing from them, but it was futile, the storm was moving too fast. The clouds embraced the giant skyscrapers and rolled towards the superheroes. They were only seconds away.

Toby tore his gaze back to the pieces of the Temporal Dilator. He loved puzzles, although he'd prefer not to be under the pressure of having the world end if he couldn't put one together. Then he got it; it was remarkably simple.

He slid the gem between the tendril fingers of one artefact. It was a perfect fit. The second 'squid' fitted perfectly on the other end, the tendrils forming a cage around the gem. It all locked into place with a smooth click of exquisite craftsmanship. The gem began to glow a gentle amber colour. Jen picked up the T-piece.

'What about this?'

Toby's answer was sucked away as the Time-Storm swept over them. There was a sudden and total silence.

Toby opened his eyes. The stillness was so intense he could hear the blood pounding in his ears. He looked around and could see the cloud receding. He was inside

# Nicking Time

the Time-Storm. Jen was next to him. They both seemed fine.

'What happened?' Her voice sounded warped and oddly out of sync with her mouth. It was like watching a badly dubbed film.

Toby noticed the waves in the Marina were frozen in place. 'We're too late,' said Toby. 'The whole city has gone. And us with it.'

'But we're not dead?'

'No, child.' They spun round to see Lord Eon standing at the end of the boardwalk, impeccably dressed as ever. 'You are my eternal prisoners. You exist, like me, in between the ticks of the clock.'

'He's feeding off our chronons,' said Toby.

Eon rolled his eyes. 'Ah, science is always so unpoetic!'

'You mean you're feeding off our own personal time,' said Jen recalling her briefing.

Eon nodded.

'But we can still fight you,' said Toby. He flicked his fingers at Eon—and nothing happened. He blinked in surprise and flicked again.

'Ah, superheroes. You are all so failingly reliant on your powers. Here they do not exist. It takes nanoseconds for your brains to command the powers and for them to manifest. Here, no such unit of time exists. Therefore your powers are *useless.*'

Jen tried to use hers, but had the same results. Toby looked at Pete—whatever was swirling in his system had stopped and he now looked like the good old Pete, weedy and unthreatening. He groaned as he stood up; the paralysis had worn off.

Toby held up the assembled artefact. 'We still have this.'

A flicker across Eon's face betrayed uncertainty. 'A useless trifle, I am afraid. I have destroyed part of the Temporal Dilator. It cannot work.'

'And we recreated it,' said Jen with a smile.

Toby took a step forward and Eon instinctively backed away. 'Do not threaten me, boy. I have mastery of time and space. I am the wielder of a Core Power. There are others like me whose skill taps into the major forces in the universe. We are unstoppable. And this day, I win. I control time; I control eternity!'

Toby took another step forward with the artefact. Eon stepped back again.

'And this gizmo can take it all away. It can suck every chronon from your body and render you powerless.'

Lord Eon smiled, but there was a trace of fear there. 'You cannot work out how to use it, or you already would have.' Toby's expression told Eon all he needed to know. 'And would you really risk the life of your friend to try?'

Pete suddenly screamed. Toby and Jen spun round to

see him hoisted into the air by an invisible hand, his arms pinned to his side. The air shimmered next to him—then the landscape around it distorted and formed a swirling gravastar. There was no dramatic hurricane force wind or thunderous noise, only Pete's screams as his skin stretched like rubber as he slowly moved closer to the vortex. He looked like a cartoon character as his entire body was pulled, an atom at a time, towards the black hole.

'Tobe! Help me!' screamed Pete. 'I'm sorry! Please! I don't want to die!'

Toby took a step towards his friend, but Jen held him back and shook her head.

'Toby! Please!' wailed Pete. His voice registered intense pain.

Tears rolled down Toby's cheeks. He turned to Eon, who was smiling.

'Drop the artefact into the portal and your friend lives. If you don't then you will watch him die and I will still get the artefact. And as punishment I will let you live. Your eternal feeling of guilt and shame will cause more pain than I could administer.'

Toby stepped towards Pete, but again he felt Jen's hand squeeze his shoulder.

Pete's entire body was hideously warped—he looked like a fine watercolour painting that had had liquid thrown across it.

'Tobe . . . I'm sorry . . . I don't want to die like this . . .'

A shudder ran through Toby's body. Should he abandon him, like Pete had done to him in Mexico? He shrugged Jen off and turned back to Eon.

'I can't let you kill him. He's still my mate no matter how much we've been fighting.'

'Toby! No!' screamed Jen. She reached for him again, but Toby pushed her away. He cradled the heavy assembled Temporal Dilator with one arm. 'This is yours, Eon. For ever.'

Lord Eon's brow knitted at the odd comment. He caught Toby's hand moving as he rammed the T-piece into a narrow hole at the end of the Dilator.

Toby had spotted the hole just before Eon had materialized. It was the only place for the T-bar to go and it fitted like a key in a lock. He heard it click and twisted the spar.

The artefact grew so bright he was forced to drop it as he shielded his eyes. He heard Eon scream—but he could also hear Pete's tormented agony.

The entire world seemed to buckle then his ears popped and Eon, the vortex, and the Time-Storm simply vanished.

Toby dropped to his knees, exhausted. Jen was at his side.

'You did it!'

# Nicking Time

Toby looked around the city. It seemed normal. The storm had vanished. People walked past with confused looks, but to them Eon's appearance had been a nano-second blip in time. The only after-effect they suffered was an intense feeling of déjà vu.

The artefact lay on the boardwalk, smouldering slightly. Toby looked around. There was no sign of Pete.

Jen laid a hand on his shoulder.

'Toby, I'm sorry. But you did the right thing. You couldn't spare the life of your friend, or anyone else, if it was weighed against saving the world.'

Toby couldn't speak. He was crushed with grief. He had killed his best friend.

The next twenty-four hours were a blur, mostly because fatigue caught up with Toby's sorrow. Eric Kirby himself had teleported to the scene and an Enforcer unit had cleared away the Temporal Dilator.

Kirby had tried to explain to Toby that Eon was trapped in the crystal, and it was being returned to Diablo Island, but Toby was uninterested in the details.

Kirby had teleported Jen and Toby back to the Foundation headquarters, the real one this time. Toby refused to say a word to defend himself, so Jen had to explain how Toby had been kidnapped from the

hospital when both he and Kirby were knocked unconscious.

Kirby relayed some of the facts from their investiga-
tion of the incident. The man with the strange eyes
who had originally stormed the hospital and caused the
whole incident had been under Momentum's control.
But it seemed that he had been working with Jake
Hunter on a plan to free Pete from the Foundation hospital. The numbers he had muttered were linked to a
subliminal recording they found playing in Pete's ward.
It was an elaborate code, delivered under hypnosis, to
ensure Pete had full control of his powers the moment
he woke from the coma.

The Council had known that Toby was one of
the Foundation's rising stars. It seems they hatched
their elaborate plan to see if they could control him
and ensure they could gather the Temporal Dilator
to stop Lord Eon. The Council couldn't trust anybody
from their own ranks and when they had tried to use
Downloaders, well, Toby had witnessed their incompe-
tence first-hand in Germany. By convincing Toby he
was working for the Foundation they had used his
scrupulous morals to do their dirty work.

With Eon's powers at their disposal, the Council
of Evil could have made life truly terrible. Fortunately, there had been a lot of internal problems at
the Council of Evil. Caused in part by Jake Hunter.

# Nicking Time

Eventually Toby decided to speak. He told them about his encounter with Eric Kirby in the past. Kirby nodded, confirming Toby's story.

'It was all part of Eon's elaborate plan to make sure he was freed from Diablo Island. Controlling events now to affect the past. Rather ingenious, but probably very easy if you can manipulate time.' Kirby looked thoughtful, then smiled and placed a friendly hand on Toby's shoulder. 'I should never have doubted your loyalty. And I should say thank you for saving me all those years ago.'

Toby didn't reply. He had lost too many things. Kirby picked up on his thoughts.

'Come with me,' he said simply.

They had made their way through the Foundation hospital, past the wards that were still being reconstructed after Pete's rampage. Kirby opened a door and placed a finger over his lips.

Toby looked inside and his heart skipped a beat. Emily was lying on a bed, fast asleep. He resisted the temptation to run over and wake her. He stepped quietly inside.

'Is she OK?' he whispered.

'Perfectly fine, if a little disorientated. She reappeared right where you left her in Germany. Unfortunately that was right in the middle of a busy autobahn, but she's OK.'

'And Lorna?'

Kirby looked hard at him. 'She has got herself caught up with Jake Hunter, I'm afraid. She is alive, but the circumstances are *complicated*. Rest assured we have our best agents dealing with the situation.'

'I've got to help her.'

'You may be too late for that. Since you have been missing, presumed rogue, she has been very upset. Those events are another tale that is coming to an end.'

Kirby's mobile phone chimed, interrupting Toby's next question. He ushered them all from Emily's room and took the video call.

A young woman appeared on the screen, wearing a headset. Behind her was the bustling activity of a Foundation control centre. 'Sir, we have picked up the signal you requested. We have a security camera feed.'

'Put it through,' commanded Kirby. He angled the phone so Toby and Jen could see.

A video clip streamed through. It was footage taken from a security camera hung in the corner of a bank. Toby watched as a supervillain smashed through the door and fired streamers of energy. Then the camera went black.

'Who was that?'

Kirby used his finger to scrub back through the

footage and froze the picture. It was blurred, but there was no mistaking—

'Pete?' exclaimed Toby. Kirby nodded grimly. 'But how? I thought . . . we saw . . .'

'You saw him vanish. I suspected that you managed to defeat Eon before he killed Pete, but I couldn't prove it. For the last twenty-four hours we have been trying to locate Pete's CUCI. Unlike you, he still possesses ours.'

The guilt Toby had been feeling washed away. He laughed, releasing the tension that had been brewing inside.

'He's alive!'

'He's alive all right. But it appears he's still on the villains' side.'

'Pete's not evil,' snapped Toby. He had no idea why he was defending his ex-friend who had attacked him and betrayed him on numerous occasions.

'Maybe not,' said Kirby. 'But he is seriously misguided. We may be able to get him back, but I do believe he is still *your* problem.'

Toby was already thinking one step ahead. He knew Kirby would want him to track down his old friend, but Toby had other ideas. The Council of Evil had used him, warped Pete, and lured his sister away.

'If I go after Pete, that's not really the root of the problem, is it?'

'Correct. But as you know, the Council of Evil, no matter how much it seems ready to implode with all its internal feuds, is still a powerful force. And more importantly, we have no idea where it is located.'

Toby pulled a crumpled map from his jacket and spread it against the wall. It was the one he had stolen from the office in the COE Headquarters. He tapped the GPS co-ordinates on the paper.

'We know *now*.'

Kirby stared at the map in astonishment. Toby noticed that Jen was smiling broadly.

It was time for payback.

Andy Briggs was born in Liverpool, England. Having endured many careers, ranging from pizza delivery and running his own multimedia company to teaching IT and film-making (though not all at the same time), he eventually remembered the constant encouragement he had received at an early age about his writing. That led him to launch himself on a poor, unsuspecting Hollywood. In between having fun writing movie scripts, Andy now has far too much fun writing novels.

He lives in a secret lair somewhere in the south-east of England—attempting to work despite his three crazy cats. His claims about possessing superpowers may be somewhat exaggerated . . .

*Crisis Point* is his third novel in the fiendishly clever 'Hero.com' series, and follows *Council of Evil*, *Dark Hunter*, and *Power Surge* in the deviously dark 'Villain.net' anti-series.